GO DEEP

GO DEEP

A SINISTER PLOT IS AFOOT TO BLOW UP THE STADIUM OF THE WORLD-CHAMPION NEW ENGLAND PIRATES.

A NOVEL BY **TERRY BOONE** AND **THOMAS R. PERO**

2019

First Edition

Library of Congress Cataloging-in-Publication Data
Boone, Terry and Pero, Thomas R.
Go deep: a novel./Terry Boone and Thomas R. Pero.—1st edition
p. cm.
ISBN 9780996239776
I. Title.
Library of Congress Control Number: 2019905619

Cover design by Harp and Company
Interior design by Creative Publishing Book Design

Published jointly by Three Rivers Group, Post Office Box 885, Norwich, Vermont 05055 and Wild River Press, Post Office Box 13360, Mill Creek, Washington 98082 USA

Wild River Press website address: www.wildriverpress.com
Book website address: www.biffgodeep.com

Printed in the United States of America

10 9 8 7 6 5 4 3 2

A Note From the Authors to the Reader

This is a work of fiction. Names, places, events, timelines, distances and other information have been adapted or created entirely by the authors. Any similarity to real people and real events is coincidental.

This book is for Karen, who *really* likes
Tony Kornheiser and Michael Wilbon—
and maybe the occasional football game.

And also for Kate, who wouldn't be caught
dead in the stands on the 50-yard line, with
or without a dyed miniature pet horse.

1

THE SHRINE

Lieutenant Francis X. "Frank" Sullivan shifted his eyes from the computer screen and looked up. Monday morning, State Police Troop H-3 barracks, 136 Washington Street, Foxborough, Massachusetts. He was reading the box score from yesterday's Red Sox game. Placing his paper cup of lukewarm Dunkin coffee on the desk, he extended his right hand.

"Trooper Egan, I presume?"

"Yes, sir, reporting for duty."

"Frank Sullivan. Welcome aboard." He got up and started for the door, thinking that she could be his daughter. Chestnut hair pulled back into a no-nonsense bun under the wide-brim Trooper's hat, she had a firm handshake.

Diminutive, maybe five-three, Julie Egan had graduated first in her class at the State Police Academy in New Braintree, out there in the middle of nowhere, near the Quabbin Reservoir.

Seeing Sullivan in person for the first time, she thought that he looked like an aging Jack Lemmon from some old movie.

Egan had been assigned to the Homeland Security Division of the Massachusetts State Police; Sullivan had spent nearly 20 years in Field Services. She started at a salary of $92,478; he was one of a couple hundred out of a couple thousand statewide who made twice that. Over a quarter-million bucks in annual payroll heading for the parking lot.

Sullivan turned the ignition key in the two-year-old dark-blue Ford Expedition, accented with the medium-blue hood, roof and doors. He waited for the traffic to pass on the Boston-Providence Highway, also known as U.S. Route 1, stretching from the mangroves of the Florida Keys all the way to the potato fields of northern Maine.

Two miles north of the barracks, Sullivan flipped the signal indicator and took a right turn.

"So, *this* is the Fox Bowl?" Egan said. "Home of the world-champion New England Pirates. The shrine."

Sullivan thought that he detected a hint of sarcasm. Bringing the vehicle to a full stop, he turned off the engine.

Passenger window down, Trooper Egan rested her fore-arms on the door of the electronics-packed official SUV and adjusted her Zeiss Terra ED 10x42 binoculars.

"Yours?" Frank asked.

"Yes. Anti-reflective coated lens lets you see detail even in low light," she said.

"A few bucks, eh?"

"Close to a grand. But worth every cent."

She began scanning the vast parking area, head slowly moving left to right. "Jesus. How many cars does this place hold?"

Sullivan explained that there are more than two dozen lots: separate areas for players, media, big shots' limos, tour buses, the stadium staff, groundskeepers, concession workers—you name it. "You're looking at only part of the many general-admission lots. Forty bucks a pop."

Egan abruptly stopped scanning, like a hunter on safari when the kudu is spotted.

"There's a . . . camouflage tower!" she exclaimed. "And there's a guy *sitting* in it."

"That's Jack the Cabbie," said Sullivan.

"He's wearing a Yankees cap," she said, adjusting the focus.

"Yeah. Probably wearing his authentic pin-striped jersey with custom lettering, *FOLLOW THE MONEY*," Sullivan laughed. "Had it made by an outfit in Seattle, Ebbetts Field Flannels or something like that."

"How does he get away with wearing that *here*?"

"Same way gangs of Townies get away with hiring a charter bus south, consuming *way* too many beers during the ride, and four hours later pile out in the Bronx, pissing on the tires and chanting 'Yankees Suck!' Strength in numbers," he added.

"But this guy appears to be up there by himself."

"Yep. You don't see anyone else around, right? Last game here was months ago." Sullivan chuckled again, then went on. "Plus, Jack is a team of one. He is his own road show. They broke the mold."

Egan held her binoculars at rest and stared at Sullivan.

"And here's some fun news," he went on. "Part of your job is going to be working with him."

2

CHOWDAH

Pulling out of Pirate Place back onto Route 1, Sullivan continued north, did a U-turn and headed south for half a mile, slowed and pulled the full-size SUV into a bumpy parking lot. The roadside sign advertised RED WING in large red letters with the silhouette of a bird's wing on top of the sign.

The sign also promised FRIED CLAMS, ITALIAN-AMERICAN FOOD, PIZZA, LIQUORS.

The two officers entered a small, ordinary looking white clapboard-sided building. It looked like it had been there a while. Egan followed Sullivan into the bar area. Scoping it out, she thought it resembled an old-fashioned railroad car, only more spacious.

Taking a seat at one of the counter stools, Egan glanced up at the copper ceiling, then placed a hand on the wooden counter with deeply worn grooves at each place, where God knows how many customers had rested their forearms and elbows—for, what, 80 years?—while waiting for their succulent fried clams.

Julie Egan, Mass State *Trooper* Egan, was momentarily lost in thought. Crisp new blue-gray uniform, leather holster holding a Smith & Wesson short-recoil locked breech .45 semi-auto. She called up the image of the famous 1958 Norman Rockwell painting depicting a friendly state trooper with a little runaway kid seated on the lunch-counter stool next to him. *Her* uniform, all these years later, almost identical to his.

"Rita, meet Trooper Egan," Frank Sullivan announced.

"Pleased to meet you, honey," the woman said. Pencil hovering over the small order pad, she added, "Don't believe half of what this bum tells you."

"She's joining us here at the happy, hopping H-3," Sullivan said. "Her specialty is tracking down terrorists."

"No need to track 'em down, hon. Just *wait* for a Sunday game to end. Then you can watch every damn idiot with a spray-painted overflowing belly, a dyed mohawk and strapped-on goat horns." She gestured with her pencil, "They're lining up in the parking lot to get in."

"Bud, what'll ya have?" Rita never called him Frank; it was always Bud.

"The usual: cuppa chowdah and a roll."

"Strips or whole?"

"Whole clam. Celebrating today. Just one more month to go, then I'll be up to my waist in the surf at midnight again, casting for stripers at Squibby. On the Vineyard."

"I'll have the same," Julie said, offering a polite smile.

Starched-white waitress uniform looking fresh, Rita came back to the counter and placed some flatware in front of both Sullivan and Egan, then brought two mugs of steaming coffee.

"So, tell me about Jack the Cabbie. *Straight* scoop," Julie said, reaching for her mug.

"Three months ago, Framingham assigned him to us," Sullivan began. "They told us it was part of a suspended sentence in some kind of sex-ring case."

"Oh, great."

"No, no, it's not that—Jack's a good guy."

Sullivan offered that, as best he understood, Jack the Cabbie had somehow become tangled up in a scheme paring up teenage virgin males with imaginatively alluring women.

"I don't think he was actually involved, but somehow he was on the periphery," Sullivan continued. "Eventually, Jack led cops to the ringleader: a Russian guy named Dimitri something-or-other. Guy lived on a cul-de-sac in Hopkinton. Running a fleet of Town Cars!"

The hot clam chowder arrived in little white cups. Rita placed them on the counter. Frank crunched oyster crackers over his chowder.

He explained that the "car service"—he made air quotation marks—had been moderately successful. Proms, graduations, weddings and Christmas parties, both coming and going, ultimately dumping the shitfaced partiers off at their front doorstep, then speeding away before the wife, or mother, turned on the porch light.

"But the Russian guy thought there had to be some way to fill in down time, increase the cash flow," Sullivan said. He tasted the chowder and dabbed his lips with a napkin.

"You know, instead of having those shiny, Lemon 409-smelling Town Cars just sitting there empty, he did some homework," Frank went on. "Gotta give the miscreant credit—did his prep and came up with a screwball scheme he called 'Meet the President.' For a *thousand bucks*, he'd dispatch a driver to meet some clean-cut kid at a safe location.

"The kid would plop in the back seat and find himself next to a Marilyn Monroe lookalike, dolled up in a slinky white dress and gleaming red lipstick, the air thick with her favorite, Floris Rose Geranium."

Egan put her spoon down and looked at Sullivan. "You're making this up."

Sullivan grinned and shook his head. "They would spend the day driving around the Boston area to all the President Kennedy historic sites: birthplace in Brookline, the JFK statue on the state house lawn, the Parker House Hotel where he announced for Congress back in 1946, also where he had a wild bachelor party in '53 before he married Jackie. The "tour," air quotation marks again, "included a drive by Faneuil Hall. That's where JFK gave his final speech in the 1960 presidential campaign, etcetera, etcetera.

"Finally, the driver would jump on the Southeast Distressway, I-93 South, and take the Dorchester exit to JFK Presidential Library. Once inside, the kid would watch an inspiring film and buy some trinket at the gift shop to prove to his parents that he'd been there."

Sullivan had nearly finished his chowder. After a pause, he wiped his mouth with the napkin and placed it on the counter, getting back to the story.

"When the kid emerged from the temple, he climbs into the backseat of the perfumed Town Car and the fake Marilyn, she begins singing 'Happy Birthday Mr. President,' you know, in that whispery voice, while she is slowly *pulling the kid's pants down* to his knees!"

Egan was shaking her head.

"The driver glances in the rearview mirror and the blonde's head is no longer visible," Sullivan continued. "*But* he can still see the kid, slouched back on the leather seat, eyes closed and moaning in obvious delight.

"Mission accomplished," said Sullivan, picking up the napkin and wiping his lips one final time.

Egan, swallowing the last spoonful of her own chowder, fell into a coughing spasm.

Frank signaled Rita for a glass of water.

"What pimply faced high school junior has a thousand bucks stashed away for something like *that*?" Egan finally managed to blurt out.

"Actually," Frank said, "you'd be surprised. Around here, some do."

The clam rolls appeared right on cue. Sullivan squeezed a plastic bottle of tartar sauce.

"Some of those little shits are driving brand-new BMWs. But see, what the Russian did was smart." After a pause to take a bite of his clam roll, Sullivan kept talking.

"Dimitri Putinov, or whatever, got the kids' grandfathers and uncles to *pay* for 'Meet the President.' With a gift certificate, for God's sake, including a made-up presidential seal." Egan hadn't touched her clam roll. She took another sip of water.

"See, when these older guys were teenagers, they'd go visit Grandma at Christmas in a three-decker walkup in Southie. There'd be three pictures hanging on the wall: Jesus Christ, the Pope, and JFK. It made an impression."

The parents, explained Sullivan, loved "Meet the President," because little Kevin was finally taking an interest in history; the kid came away with the thrill of his young life, thinking now that the boring ol' man at Thanksgiving is suddenly, as the kids say, *epic.*

And Kevin was certain to keep his mouth shut. Frank paused for another bite. Three quick chews and he went on. "Probably wondering what other exciting surprises Uncle Danny or Grandpa Roy had up his sleeve for graduation."

"But statutory rape in this state is *16*," Julie exaggerated, as she started on her toasted clam roll.

"Yes," replied Lieutenant Frank Sullivan, "but MGL c.272 says it's still against the law to *induce* a person under 18 into having sex if he is of a, quote, unquote, chaste life. Well, hell, nowadays," opined Frank, "there are plenty of horny high-school boys who can't get laid to save themselves. 'Dating' is reduced to cellphone porn or joining a marauding herd of vaping teenage chicks hanging out at some vacant mall."

He watched Egan as she ate.

"Anyway, *that* is how they nailed his fat Russian ass," Frank said. "Dimitri was facing up to three years."

"What happened to him?"

"No one really knows. He skipped bail—a million bucks—and was caught on camera at the Mass Pike-495 toll booth heading south. The very *next* day, New York City detectives responded to our APB with a report that a squat, heavyset male fitting the description was seen entering Trump Tower. They staked out Fifth Avenue for a week but never saw the guy again.

"And by the way," Sullivan added, toothpick clenched in his teeth as he held open the door of the diner for Julie to exit, "When you eventually meet Jack the Cabbie, you don't know *any* of this, okay? And you *do not* go asking him any personal questions. Got it?"

Trooper Julie Egan nodded.

"Talk to him about trout fishing in Montana. Or tying flies. Baseball, *anything*!"

3

BRANDI

The parking wasn't easy, but Whitey preferred this Dunkin Donuts over the four other locations within five minutes of his condo. He clicked the locks on the Corvette and headed for the entrance. There it was, white letters across the orange plastic facade above the front door: Original Dunkin' Location—Established 1950.

Christ. Two lifetimes ago. His ol' man woulda been a teenager. Then again, Whitey was pretty sure there were no Dunkin Donuts franchises anywhere in Louisiana back in the day. He did recall at least one in Lake Charles last time he visited.

He ordered an extra-large Dunkaccino with two Turbo Shots of espresso. After he'd paid the sweet thing, Brandi, multi-tasking at the register, Whitey turned to leave and was stopped like a rookie safety knocked on his ass when he misread the play.

Someone had taped a large poster on the wall near the men's room. Right there, a foot in front of him, was the iconic bright red lips and tongue of The Rolling Stones. A concert poster. The only New England stop on the tour. Tickets on sale now, if there were any left.

Whitey took a big pull on the straw, swallowed maybe one of the Turbot Shots in the first gulp and continued staring at the poster. He was not a big fan of the Stones. Shit, they were really old. He thought again about his dad as a teenager.

What intrigued him was the venue listed on the poster—the Fox Bowl. *"Gratter mes boules,"* he whispered to himself, unconsciously rubbing his crotch.

Whitey backed away from the poster and slowly lowered himself into a chair. He fumbled the XL Dunkaccino onto a table behind him, almost dropping it to the floor in the process, and continued looking at the poster.

After a few long seconds, he slowly gave another suck on the straw and glanced back toward the counter. Brandi was still giving him the eye and the smile as she talked into her headset mic to a drive-thru customer. He grinned back and gave her a wink.

The fucking Fox Bowl! All the Sunday afternoons he'd spent on the artificial turf, all the passes he'd caught, the 3,904 yards he'd covered on that field alone, the crowd noise, the trash talk with guys who tried to cover him. *Now* they're bringing in geriatric British-white rockers to generate even more fucking revenue.

Whitey remembered a big defensive tackle he'd played with in New Orleans his first year in pro football. Kilian "Killer" Murray. Every time they won a game, especially if Murray had made at least one sack, he would proclaim to anyone within earshot of his locker, "Pleased to meet you, hope you guess my name," from the Stones' *Sympathy for the Devil.*

Wonder where the Killer is now? Was he screwed by some coach or owner who decided the salary was too high and time for this hunk of flesh to move on? Early retirement for you, pal. We have a new crop all ready to take your slot. It's just business.

Never mind we play our ass off and they sell more tickets, rake in the TV money, peddle the jerseys, cups, license plates, anything else with a team logo.

You're done here, son. Under the bus you go. Sorry.

Fuck that! How do you get even-up when *they* are still picking up all the *chips* on the table, and *you* are sitting in a Dunkin Donuts mumbling to yourself?

And checking out Brandi with purple and pink stripes in her Day-Glo platinum hair.

Shauntay finds out you looking at this white chick, you be the one havin purple and pink stripes on your ass, bro.

Whitey got up, touched the poster with his right hand, smack on the red lips and tongue, looked back one more time at Brandi, gave her both a smile and the index finger pistol shot, then headed for his car.

The Mut & Callahan Show was just ending on WEEI. Whitey turned off the radio, backed out onto the street and was damn near T-boned by a MBTA bus.

Holy shit! The blaring horn from the bus nearly caused him to piss his pants. Asshole probably loves scaring the bejesus out of innocent drivers.

It took a few seconds for Whitey to calm down. Carefully pulling the car around and heading toward Morrison Street, he would take his time driving into the city. What's the hurry? She's out shopping already this morning and we'll be looking at one more fashion show before lunch time. And how much will *that* fucking cost?

That last thought brought him back around to: No future paychecks in sight, *no* prospects with any new team. And *no* invitations to put on a blazer, join some piddly-ass TV sports show then *rave* about all his ol' buddies still playing with the New England fucking Pirates.

Taking the I-93 north ramp to Boston, Whitey watched for traffic coming up behind him. He carefully merged left, brought the 'vette up to 65 and tapped the cruise-control button. There goes another big ass bus blowing right by him.

The echo from the horn two minutes earlier was still in his ears.

"Guy drives like that," Whitey said to himself, "probably a close pal or related to Coach Willy."

4

BOOM-BOOM

Shauntay was, in fact, shopping. Shimmy & Silk was not at the top of her list of Newbury Street establishments in Boston's fashionable Back Bay neighborhood. But despite the name, they always had a great selection of denim.

Summer was coming and that called for new jeans.

After only an hour in the store, she found three pair of skinny jeans in different styles—ankle length, scissor slit and high rise—at $248 each. Out came the platinum card.

Walking back to the apartment, Shauntay stopped in front of her favorite store, The Shoe Boutique, and retrieved her iPhone from the Saint Laurent bag hanging off her right shoulder. Speed dial to Whitey. Was he there yet?

"Hey," he answered on the first ring.

"You are *not* feeding my baby those munchy things," she said.

"Baby" was a three-year-old Pomeranian named Jasmine. Those "munchy things" were jelly-filled doughnut hole treats. Whitey had once made the mistake of allowing Shauntay to observe him feeding the treat to her dog. Had it been a TV reality show, the next scene would most definitely have featured much yelling at Whitey and a quick trip to a vet's emergency room, even though the dog had *not* shown signs of unfavorable reaction.

"I don't do that no more," he lied. "She's fine. Standing here in the window waitin for Mama to come home."

"Good girl. Just one more stop. I'll be back," she looked at her watch, "before noon."

Whitey looked at his watch; 10:52. "Not going anywhere," he said.

Shauntay gave him the kiss-kiss sound and ended the call.

Whitey had been watching Big Ten Wrestling on the flat screen mounted above the breakfast counter in the kitchen. The volume was on mute. Two heavyweights in head gear, relaxed and staring at one another during an official time out. A referee, off to one side, was watching a video replay.

"This can't be real," Whitey said, shaking his head.

You pin your opponent to the mat and they want to review it?

He picked up the remote and began channel surfing. After eight or nine clicks, he stopped and went back two channels. It was slow motion footage of a multi-story building collapsing in some controlled demolition exercise. There were guys in hard hats pointing and talking with a reporter.

Whitey laughed. "*Blow up* this old house," he said to Jasmine, who was now standing on the counter looking up at him.

"Sorry, kid. Munchies all gone." Whitey brought up the volume.

Forty-five minutes later, when Shauntay opened the door, Whitey was engrossed in the program that had now covered five different implosions. The guy in charge, one of two brothers who ran this demolition company, was explaining all of the steps required in planning each job.

Whitey turned to see Shauntay coming into the apartment. He hit the power button on the remote turning off the TV. Jasmine was off the counter and running to Mama.

"Boom," Whitey whispered to himself.

Following 15 minutes of showing off her new jeans in a barefoot-and-bare-breasted solo fashion show for Whitey, Shauntay led her man through a spirited "nooner." It was first and goal before he knew it. Slow it down. Too late. Penalty, delay of game. And the whole event lasted approximately the same number of minutes as a commercial break in the halftime show of a Sunday game on TV.

Now, still naked, she was trying to arouse his attention regarding her extensive collection of shoes, carefully arranged inside a large closet approximately two short yards from the bed. Whitey seemed to be lost in the huddle.

"Boom-Boom. *Look* at me," she said, standing in front of him wearing only a pair of dark chambray platform heels. The shoes had four-and-a-half-inch stacked-wedge heels, a one-and-a-half-inch platform and a roller buckle closure back strap.

Whitey turned to face Shauntay, looked down at her shoes, made the OK sign with his left hand and said, *"magnifique."* It sounded more like mug'niffik. Averting his eyes, he went back to his thoughts of the moment. It wasn't as though he hadn't seen *that* pair, or any of the maybe 100-plus other friggin pairs of shoes. And it wasn't like he'd failed to recall the obscene amounts she regularly produced on credit card statements. He just wasn't into shoes. Even on a knockout, naked woman.

Now she was leaning over him, whispering. "Boom," she said, her breasts grazing the top of his head as she rubbed a finger on his right ear. "You *not* thinking about those sweet young things at the mall?" It was more of a command than a question. Two points here: Shauntay was the only person to call Whitey "Boom-Boom," a nickname she gave his penis. And he wasn't even thinking of Brandi with the pink and purple stripes.

Increasingly enveloping Whitey's brain right now were thoughts about blowing things up—or, as the guy in the TV documentary called it, "imploding structures."

A quick, double-bark slightly above 60 decibels. Jasmine was outside the bedroom and wanted attention. "Mama's coming, baby," Shauntay said. Whitey let that one go. She went to let the dog come into the room while he went to the shower.

Thirty minutes later, Shauntay said that she was going to take Jasmine for a long walk. Whitey said that he needed to go back to his condo in Quincy and would return in time for them to go out for dinner.

"Seven-thirty, baby," he said, giving Shauntay a kiss and the imaginary pistol shot to Jasmine. In the back of his mind, Whitey knew that he was going to suck it up and miss the semi-final round of the college basketball tournament on TV tonight.

5

NOW THE FORECAST

Sunday and Monday turned out sunny and unseasonably cold. The weather didn't stop people from walking, jogging, biking, flying kites, playing frisbee and jumping at any chance to be outside. It really had been a pissy winter.

A large number of the people outside wore ear buds, some wireless and others connected to a thin, plastic-coated wire attached to a battery-operated device. Hell, some of the devices may have been solar-powered.

If you could stop each person and ask, "What're you listening to?," you might get a sense of the information and entertainment offerings available to the average citizen in the metropolitan region known as Greater Boston, New England's most populous city, ranked sixth in the U.S. combined statistical areas with over eight million people.

And more than 100 radio signals in the region, AM and FM, *not* including low-power (LP) community stations or satellite channels.

From Beethoven to baseball, wasabi recipes to weather patterns, among the daily audio treats there was no shortage of call-in shows. One might be forgiven for recalling the observation made by long ago Boston newspaper columnist George Frazier, in which he opined that one of the first things encouraged for those recently released from mental institutions was that they phone the local radio station and have at it.

Of course, that was a long time ago. Things have changed, some good and some, well, not so good.

On one of those LP stations, nobody was really certain *where* it was broadcasting from, a one-man, two-hour show, produced, hosted and engineered by a guy who changed his name every night, focused strictly on weather and football. It could be September, January or July, if a caller brought up anything *other* than football or the weather, it took the what's-his-name host two seconds to dismiss the call. Never mind that the Sox were fresh into a new season, that the Celtics and Bruins still had remaining games on their calendars—you weren't going to discuss it on this show.

"Now the Forecast. Go ahead, you're on the radio," the host said. Tonight, he was using the name Jim Thorpe.

"Thanks for taking my call," a man said. "You got a good show here, uh . . . Jim."

"Appreciate it. What's on your mind?"

"I wanna talk about the Pirates. And, uh, Biff's new contract."

"Hail Mary and pull out the stops. My boy, Biff. What is it, you have a problem with the 'reported' contract?"

Caller: "Nah. I don't give a damn how much they're paying him. He sells a lot of tickets, creates jobs and income for a buncha people. That's all good. I get it."

"So, what's your beef with Biff?" Sound effect of crowd groaning in unison.

"Uh, well, don't ya think it's time that maybe somebody else got to play?"

Before the caller could go on, without a verbal response from the program host, the radio erupted with an all-male chorus singing the refrain "You can wear the crown" from the old football fight song, *Buckle Down, Winsocki,* a 1940s number that had been a fall Saturday afternoon staple on radio stations all around the country.

Sitting alert in his rig outside the Revere Hotel on Stuart Street, just off the Common, Jack the Cabbie had been singing along with the fight song. When it finished, he said to himself, "Sis Boom Bah."

Whitey LeBlanc was also listening to the show. He'd never heard the song before and wondered where Winsocki College was located.

"It's a *Monday night* in Beantown and *you* are on the radio. Now the Forecast. From Brookline. Hello, what's on your mind?"

Woman caller: "Hi. Would it be okay if I told your listeners about a fundraiser for my daughter's lacrosse team?"

Click. She was gone.

"Sorry, dear," said Jim Thorpe. "Send it to *The Globe*."

Next caller: "Hey, Jim. Thanks for the fight song. Love it. Listen, all this BS about Biff, he's got attitude, talent, skills, experience. For cryin out loud, whadda people want? I say if he can play til he's 50, great!"

Ding—the ubiquitous bell sound used throughout the show when a caller made a point the host happened to agree with. But this caller was also dumped without another peep.

"We have time for one more call," Jim said. "Now the Forecast. What's up in Springfield?"

A man's voice that sounded as though he might be constipated: "It's nonsense. All these prima donnas—football, baseball, basketball, hockey. They're pampered, overpaid and over-rated. I think your show should stick to the weather. And global warming."

Click. That caller was gone. Theme music from *Jaws* came up under the host's voice. "And *that,* kiddos, will do it for another gut-wrenching saga from right here, the electro-magnetic center of the universe. But, before we go, a comment and a question for our last caller. Listen up! *One*, you didn't mention soccer. And, *two*, have you ever *played* a sport . . . in your entire life?"

Theme music took the show to 8:59:45, when Jim Thorpe signed off: "Tomorrow night, Otto Graham will be our host. Charge the phone and tune in."

6

DOOR'S OPEN

A velocity yellow Corvette Z06 with Massachusetts "The Spirit of America" vanity plates, GO DEEP, pulled into the cracked blacktop parking area of a run-down 1950s-era motel. Neon signage:

Free HBO

Ask About Our Weekly Rates

Sorry, We Have Vacancies!

Location, location, location. The motel was directly across the highway from the Silver Slipper, a gentleman's club in Danvers.

The driver's door swung open and out stepped Whitey LeBlanc. Yet he wasn't instantly identifiable, primarily because he was wearing a desert-tan camouflage ski mask.

He sauntered around to the rear of the car, popped the trunk, reached in and grabbed a colored string tethering one of the red Mylar heart-shaped balloons expressing the sentiment, YOU'RE SO SPECIAL, in white letters. He sucked in a long whiff of helium from the balloon.

At the entrance to Room 9, Whitey gave a soft rap with his knuckles: three knocks.

"Door's open," said a hoarse voice from inside the room.

The tarnished brass knob was ringed with dark, greasy stains. Whitey turned it gingerly and stepped into the room.

"Mr. Mayor?" he announced in a high, squeaky voice.

"Welcome to my office," answered a voice from a tiny bathroom next to a closet. The voice presumably belonged to the individual with very hairy legs, pants down around his ankles.

Rewind to three nights earlier at a dimly lit French restaurant and a trip to the *toilettes pour hommes.* Slipping a crisp Ben Franklin to François the *maître d'*, Whitey had asked for a confidential lead. He knew very well that he could trust François, both for discretion and reliability.

Later the same evening, when removing his camel hair overcoat at Shauntay's way-too-expensive apartment, he found a note in a pocket. It was written on a card of textured parchment, cursive hand with old-fashioned fountain-pen black ink: The Mayor of Somerville, 617-590-2144.

The Mayor of Somerville? Whitey wondered. How in hell is *he* going to help me?

But François had never steered him wrong. So, the next morning, he called the number on the card. Which led to this meeting on this evening in Danvers.

Closing the motel room door behind him, Whitey was instantaneously blinded by a flood of LED lights, so bright he had to turn his back, which was, of course, the whole idea. "The Mayor" got this little trick from the movie, *The Thomas Crown Affair*—not the cheesy Pierce Brosnan–Rene Russo art-heist remake; the *original* 1968 with Steve McQueen and Faye Dunaway.

In fact, The Mayor knew a few of the stunt extras in the bank-robbery scene from that 50-year-old flick. It was only later that the casting director for the film came to realize that some of the "locals" chosen for their authentic, thick Boston accents, were the real deal: actual operating neighborhood hoodlums.

7

FULL MICHAEL JACKSON

"**Rocco? It's Mikey**. How ya doin? Hey, listen, I need a favor."

Rocco Rossini of Cranston, Rhode Island knew that when Michael O'Connolly of Somerville, Mass.—aka "The Mayor of Somerville"—called him: a) It wasn't very often, b) There was some serious coin in it, and c) It usually involved disposal of an inconvenient dead body. Maybe more than one.

Within 24 hours of the hastily scheduled meeting at the motel, O'Connolly discovered that his visitor was not a retired French soccer player ("*fooot*-bawl-air" named Jacques), as Whitey had pretended in his bizarre, helium-induced accent.

Getting to the facts, however, turned out to be child's play. Literally. Minutes after the poseur had driven across the street to the Silver Slipper for a lap dance or two, O'Connolly had emailed dozens of still digital photos of LeBlanc, taken while he was inside the motel room, to a colleague named Richard, who lived in Medford, the next town over from Somerville. Richard's 11-year-old son, Ricky, shy kid with a straight-A-grade average and a bank of computers in the basement, was asked to examine the images and report back to his dad.

"Sumbitch isn't French, for Christ sake," Richard told O'Connolly in a cellphone call. "Is *that* what the asshole told you? He's from some shithole in Louisiana! Went to LSU. Or, at least *played football* while he was enrolled there. Probably never attended more than two classes a month."

The guy O'Connolly had met with in the motel room, he learned, was in fact a former New England Pirates wide receiver, one Antoine "Whitey" LeBlanc, Jr. Figuring that out had been a piece of cake.

Ricky, the 11-year-old digital sleuth, enlarged several of the images and was struck by a tiny constellation of shiny refractions: a gaudy Pirates Championship ring, glittering back at the spy cameras.

"You remember him?" Richard said. "The speedy black dude who made that spectacular catch for the 70-yard touchdown just before half-time for all the marbles two years ago."

"Oh, yeah. Right," O'Connolly replied. "All-Pro something like five years in a row. Then he just seemed to disappear."

Ricky had also spotted that the man was wearing Nikes—no way "Jacques" would have been seen in anything but French Fab Enkos.

"But the best part," Richard said, laughing, "is how Whitey got his nickname."

The son had noticed that, when the man in the pictures was seen from a certain angle, the skin on his left ear and a patch on his neck appeared oddly lighter. Ricky began searching online. It didn't take long before he was nimbly scrolling through the archives of *The Advocate*, Louisiana's largest newspaper, since 1909.

Turns out the nickname "Whitey" isn't because some Cajun ancestor, probably a slave owner, was named LeBlanc.

"It's for the botched 'full Michael Jackson' treatment—skin bleach, nose job, the whole shebang. LeBlanc paid 10 grand to some scam-artist name a 'Dr. Robert,' aka Botox Bobby, operating outa some backroom vet clinic in Baton Rouge," Richard said, snorting Diet Pepsi through his nose and barely able to get the words out. "*Totally* screwed it up. Fake doc probably ended up swimming with the 'gators—real ones."

"There's the internet for ya. And some kid, that Ricky of yours," said The Mayor with genuine admiration.

8

THE HILLTOP

The Corvette seemed to know its way over the meandering lines of weeds growing through cracks in the asphalt—no need for directions to the broken-glass, neon-lit parking lot. The Hilltop Motel in all its pathetic glory. Cops don't even have a remote idea how many shadowy trysts had been consummated here over the years.

On this follow-up visit, Whitey was instructed to knock at room number 13. He approached the sun-bleached, paint-peeled steel door but stopped two feet short. Inside he could hear an argument going on.

Shit! This was supposed to be Whitey and The Mayor. *Alone*, same as before. *Back away discreetly and get the hell out of here?* No, he'd wait for a minute.

He leaned closer to the door.

"Oh, fuck *that!*" said a voice inside the room—sure *sounded* like The Mayor, same husky voice of the man he met here a week ago. At that meeting, The Mayor spent all his time talking from a relaxed perch on the toilet but didn't seem to be disguising his voice.

For his part, Whitey's previous, helium-influenced subterfuge had seemed to work out smartly, he thought, although the weird voice had proven a bit awkward when, after the meeting, he pulled across the highway for a quick beer and a couple of dances.

"Yeah, yeah, I got that, you're right. Good point. You got me there."

Whitey continued eavesdropping but couldn't make out the other voice—it was muffled. Maybe it was several voices. *What if there was a whole fucking crew in there?* Was he walking into a trap? *Shit.*

Perhaps the other guy was on speakerphone.

Nah. He wouldn't be able to hear him at all.

The Mayor kept talking, not always clearly, only when he raised his voice.

Whitey swallowed, then knocked on the door. Three quick, loud raps.

Silence.

He turned the knob slowly and pushed the door but remained outside. He was standing on a frayed, faded doormat with WELCOME TO THE HILLTOP barely legible.

"Mister Mayor?" Whitey said, now taking a tentative step through the door.

"Goddamn right get rid of em!" said the stout, balding man. He was lying on a thin paisley bedspread in black stocking feet. Whitey recognized the same hairy legs from a week ago. A pair of pink boxer shorts festooned with tiny polka dot sailfish and a white T-shirt above covered his ample torso.

The man looked up and saw Whitey. He waved him in with one hand and poured a drink with the other, another Gentleman Jack on the rocks. The bottle was a third empty.

As the gauzy scene slowly came into focus, Whitey became aware that the television was on. The Mayor had been carrying on a conversation with the damn TV! Across the bottom of the screen the Fox News chiron, the so-called crawl, read in bold red letters: AMERICA'S MARCH TOWARD SOCIALISM. That's when he heard Sean Hannity's voice: "Should we start reducing the number of women in Congress? Tweet yes or no. You decide."

The Mayor bellowed, "For Christ sake, *yes*, every single one of em—*the liberal bitches!*" And then instantaneously, like a miniature volcano suddenly erupting, a firehose of orange flame spewed out from a short 12-gauge 20-inch pump-action shotgun, lighting up the darkened room. *BOOM!*

Ten feet away, opposite the bed, the mirror over a desk exploded in a violent spray of flying glass shards.

Through the acrid haze of smoke from the gun, Whitey could see a light space surrounded by a yellow wall stained from decades of cigarette smoke.

Frozen in place, only his eyes dared to blink. *Holy fuckin shit—this guy's insane.* All that he could bring himself to do was to stare at the spot where the mirror had been a split-second earlier.

On the right, taped to the wall and framed by dangling glass, was a faded poster of the 1967 Red Sox and a smaller painting of the Virgin Mary. The poster was signed; the religious keepsake was not.

Whitey slowly turned his head left toward the bed. The Mayor ejected the smoking plastic shotgun shell from the chamber and was reaching into a bucket of Chick-fil-A.

"That's my idea of a tweet!" the Mayor said through a lingering smoker's cough, clearly pleased with himself. Then he leaned against the filthy backboard and began laughing uproariously, ending in a coyote howl at the water-stained ceiling.

Extending the bucket toward Whitey, he said, "Want something to eat?"

Statue-erect, White remained paralyzed. The Mayor looked over at the demolished mirror and frame. Hannity was still talking in the background.

"Oh, that," said The Mayor. He waved his left arm. "My girl comes in tomorrow morning. She'll take care of it."

Reaching for a piece of chicken, he added, mid-chew, "Now take off that silly mask."

9

BIKERS FOR BUDDY

It was mid-morning when Michael O'Connolly hit the highway in a southern trajectory for Little Rhody, the Ocean State, the refuge of the immortal libertarian Roger Williams, the path "The Mayor" had taken so many times over the years. He was going to meet his old friend Rocco for lunch.

"Have a Gansett, Neighbor!" He was old enough to remember the beer commercials on the AM radio broadcast of ballgames.

If anyone knew concrete, it was Rocco. He had made a bloody fortune from that elemental mixture of 15 percent cement paste, 70 percent crushed rock and 15 percent water, give or take.

Rocco Rossini got his start back in 1974, when he organized "Bikers for Buddy" in the political insurgency campaign that made mafia-prosecutor Vincent Albert "Buddy" Cianci, Jr. mayor of Providence.

O'Connolly drifted away in thought as 18-wheelers zoomed by. He smiled, recalling Rocco telling him that Cianci could have been president under the right circumstances. Son of a bitch used to show up all over the state at parades, ribbon-cutting ceremonies, weddings, christenings, graduations, clambakes, barbecues—the works. Always with the flashing-blue lights police escort and the flamboyant entrance.

Rocco said that Cianci would "jump to attend the opening of an envelope."

Shame they nailed his ass for assaulting that guy with a hunk of firewood and a lit cigarette to the eye. Accused the guy of fucking his ex-wife—his *ex-wife!* Who gives a shit? *Hot Italian blood,* Mike guessed. Still not sure exactly what happened. He knows Rocco stuck with Buddy and it paid off when the little shit came back, in what, the late '80s? Yeah, around then. Jumped back into the spotlight as radio talk show host on AM 920, WHJJ. Then all these billboards started showing up: "He never stopped caring about Providence."

And in 1991 the convicted felon was elected again! Boy, that's when things really took off for Rocco. That's when Cianci launched the "Providence Renaissance," as he liked to call it. Christ! Rocco sold Buddy on this grandiose dream to build a giant shopping mall on top of Ray's Park & Lock dirt lot. And didn't Rossini get the juicy contracts for pouring the concrete holding up 1.4 million square feet of fast-food courts and bullshit overpriced retail space? Damn. Biggest mall in Rhode Island. Set him up for life.

Watching his mirror in traffic, O'Connolly turned off I-95 at Providence Place. Instead of taking a right to wend his way to Federal Hill, though, which would have been the direct route, he veered left on Memorial Boulevard toward the city center, then over the canal on the Waterman Street bridge.

O'Connolly couldn't help himself. His emotions were drawing him to re-live a personal tradition: cruising College Hill with an eye peeled for gaggles of young women, ideally stray rich RISD students from California.

It didn't take long. O'Connolly pulled to the curb and rolled down the driver's window on his aged, weather-dulled, three-gear International Scout. On the opposite side, the passenger window was smashed and closed up with a piece of wine-box cardboard and duct tape. Not a vehicle to attract women of any age. The right rear fender was rusted and a different color from the rest of the truck. A twisted wire shirt hanger stood in for the long-gone radio antenna. To the wire hanger was tied a waving coyote tail.

"Excuse me, young ladies. I'm from out of town and I'm looking for something good to eat."

"Ah, like, what kind of food?" said a brunette in jeans, quickly adding, "There's like a rilly *dank* Persian vegan place right here on Benefit Street."

"Goddess Vegan. Just two blocks down," said her companion, a slim blonde with a backpack, pointing the way.

"Gee, that's sounds tasty. I've never dined with a goddess. But I'm pretty hungry. I been thinking 'bout a big bloody Porterhouse. You know, one of those caveman cuts with the bone all charred."

O'Connolly was giving them the evil grin.

"Right outa the fire. Coupla pounds, maybe three. They got anything like that around here? I want that sucker *mooing on the platter!*"

Mikey let loose with the coyote howl and roared away in a trail of black diesel fumes, cackling and coughing like a madman, *"Ah hah-hah-hah,"* thoroughly amused with himself.

The two girls looked at each other in bewilderment.

"Creepy," said the blonde.

"Totally creepy," her friend agreed.

The willowy young women resumed their conversation, wandering up the street into the rest of their lives.

Pulling into a space at the front of the Old Canteen on Atwells Avenue, O'Connolly parked behind a dark, shiny BMW and a white Mercedes, both convertibles.

Mike saw no good reason to drive a new vehicle. *All a luxury car does,* he thought, *is draw attention.* And unlike politicians and celebrities in and out of revolving-door rehab, he figured the less attention, the better.

He liked going old-school Italian when he met Rocco—hell, that was half the fun of coming down here. Starched white tablecloths. Gleaming glasses perfectly placed. Polite waiters in tuxes who knew your name. He always gave the parking valet a $25 tip in rumpled bills, coming and going. Some kid who was always grateful.

Rocco was seated at his usual corner table. He was in his blue striped Ermenegildo Zegna accented by a silk baby-blue tie. He rose.

"Mik*e-e-e,*" Rocco said in his smooth baritone voice.

"There he is," Mike said as they hugged each other. O'Connolly was in a gray tweed sport jacket, leather elbow patches, open collar white shirt.

"How ya doin?"

"Not bad, not bad."

The bottle of 2012 Ruffino Chianti Riserva Ducale Gold was already in the decanter. Rocco was always the gracious host.

"We'll have two orders of your Little Necks Giovanni," he told the waiter, a short man standing inconspicuously off to the side.

"Yes, Mr. Rosinni, and for the main course?"

Rocco looked at Mike.

"Please go ahead," Mike said. "Everything you order is so goddamn good!"

"Scaloppine con Fungghi a la Marsala."

"A cocktail to start, gentlemen?" the waiter asked.

"Glenmorangie with a splash of water," Rocco said.

"Gentleman Jack on the rocks," Mike said. "Make it a double."

When the waiter had gone, Rocco got straight to it.

"So, what, you got some packages for me?"

"Naw—those days are gone. I don't need anything ta *disappear* in concrete. But I do need ta have some concrete go away."

Rocco was smiling. "How much?"

"Don't know exactly, but easily as much as you poured into Providence Place."

Rocco's body stopped. He put a hand on the table. "Jesus—that's a small city!" he whispered.

"It is."

After a beat, Rocco said, "Mike, old pal, we don't do demolitions. You should know that." He looked around the room, then added, "As a matter of fact, we hire that out when we have to. And nothing on that scale."

The waiter came with the drinks. Rocco waited for him to leave again, then resumed.

"You need a demolitions expert, a real pro that specializes in making things go boom in a big way. This isn't anything to screw around with."

O'Connolly was all ears. Rocco paused and had a sip of his Scotch.

"More than a few packages under the skating rink," he said softly. "Wonder what archeologists will think."

"Maybe view them as some sort of reverential catacombs," O'Connolly offered.

"Yeah," Rossini raised his eyebrows and considered the romantic notion. "Never know."

As they talked, Rocco grew wistful, reminiscing about poker games during Buddy's last years at the Mayor's penthouse suite at the Biltmore. This was after Cianci was indicted a second time, April 2001, federal criminal charges of racketeering, conspiracy, extortion, bribery, witness tampering *and* mail fraud. He beat some of the charges, but was found guilty of racketeering, conspiracy and running a corrupt criminal enterprise. Ended up in a Federal Pen at Fort Dix down in Jersey, Sopranos country, where they call quahogs clams. "Gastronomic philistines!"

Looking at O'Connolly and quietly shaking his head, Rocco's eyes welled up. He confided that he has Buddy's toupée in a glass-dome case in a place of honor in his walk-in cigar humidor.

"A crook for the ages. But look at what he accomplished. I stop and think of that guy every time I grab a Cohiba," he said, reaching up to wipe a tear.

"I do miss the baldheaded little prick."

10

LOCATION, LOCATION, LOCATION

"**Tommy? Hey, it's Mikey**. Got a big favor to ask."

One Thomas McGuire and Michael O'Connolly went *way* back, starting with the busing riots during the 1970s. Now, it was Rocco Rossini's suggestion that Mike should find a real pro that prompted this phone call.

"I need to find someone who can blow things up. Gotta be *hundred-percent* reliable. No screwing around, ya know?" O'Connolly said.

"What 'chew gonna blow, Mikey?"

"I'm not—friend a mine. He's got a cement mixer fulla dynamite he needs to unload," he lied.

"What the fuck's he gonna do, blow up the Roman Coliseum?" Tommy said with a chuckle.

"Pert near," O'Connolly said.

"Got a pen?"

"Yeah—gah head."

"Alex C. Cahill. Friends call him AC," McGuire said. "Back from three tours in Afghanistan. Not very happy about it. Pissed off at the world. Demolitions guy. Solid. A little crazy, but solid."

"Where can I find him?"

"At the Super Wunder Mart in Walpole," McGuire said.

Now that's convenient. "Works there?"

"Lives there."

"He *lives* at Wunder Mart?" O'Connolly said.

"The *Super* Wunder Mart. Lives in a dumpster around back."

"He lives in a *dumpster* . . . at Wunder Mart?"

"Hey. *Why* do you keep repeating what I'm tellin ya?"

"Because it's *ridiculous!* Nobody can fuckin *live* at Wunder Mart," O'Connolly said.

"Actually, he's set up in one of those big corrugated metal shipping containers. You know, the kind that come over packed with cheap lawn chairs and shit."

"Okay, good. Thanks. I'll catch you later." Mikey reached under the seat to make sure the Glock 48 was there.

Fiddling with his after-market seat belt and finally making it click into place, he grabbed the worn stick-shift knob in his partially refurbished International Scout, then slowly backed out of the driveway.

A minute later, O'Connolly took the southbound exit off 128 onto I-95, the same way he had done two days earlier when he'd gone to see Rocco. Only this time he got off at exit 10, took a right on Coney Street, then a left on the old Providence Highway.

Cautiously driving through the massive parking lot, he craned his neck as he passed sign after sign:

Wunder Mart Bakery

Wunder Mart Deli

Wunder Mart Garden Center

Wunder Mart Grocery Pickup

Wunder Mart Money Center

Wunder Mart Pharmacy

Wunder Mart Photo Center

Wunder Mart Vision & Glasses

Even a Dunkin Donuts inside!

"Ah-oooo!" Mikey cocked his head back and let out the yelp. *I take it back!* he thought. *Saints preserve us. Somebody* could *move right into this place. How many years did he read the average American male now lived—78.69 years? Christ. Buy a Wunder Mart casket on layaway and be all set for the rest of em.*

Then it instantly came to him. Mikey recalled that he'd read about some Wunder Mart cashier being named "Employee of the Year" after helping a woman give birth, right there at the fucking checkout!

"I can help you over here at register 5, ma'am?"

The Mayor of Somerville took a couple spins around the small village of rusting shipping containers behind the Super Wunder Mart. He spotted the orange one, complete with the life-size vinyl Aquaman decal.

"AC" Cahill heard not a sound. However, his Protect America home electronic surveillance system alerted him; a visitor had arrived. A buzzer sounded. The steel door slid open.

O'Connolly stepped in and looked around. He saw a shaved bald head sitting in front of two 85-inch Sony LED screens, one flashing *Road Redemption* and the other *God of War.* Cahill was frenetically playing both video games simultaneously.

O'Connolly cautiously approached the man. Cahill stood and removed his headphones. Pale skin, muscular, a big lean guy with a humorless expression, he was dressed in a green T-shirt and desert camouflage cargo pants. O'Connolly guessed him to be maybe 30 years old.

"AC" motioned for O'Connolly to take a seat, gesturing to a plastic lawn chair held together with duct tape.

Mikey stared at him for a full minute before lowering himself into the chair.

"You're eating out of a dog dish," he said.

"Chocolate ice cream—want some?" AC held the bowl out to him.

"It's a *dog* dish!"

"Yeah. Sally's. She was my rescue Lab. Yellow," he said, taking another spoonful of the ice cream, then adding, "Died last winter."

O'Connolly waved his hand to decline the ice cream offer.

"Don't worry. Her bowls are like totally sterilized. Plus, did you know a dog's mouth is like . . . cleaner than ours?"

Mikey gave a patronizing smile, then handed his host a bottle of Lagavulin 16-year single-malt.

"Puritas et mentis et corporis," the ex-commando replied. Now it was his turn to wave off the offering. "But thank you anyway, dude."

Standing in place, holding the bottle of choice whisky, O'Connolly was momentarily at a loss. He glanced at the now-empty dog dish almost expecting to see the man lick the bowl.

AC stepped over to a weight-lifting bench positioned snugly against one wall of the container. There were two rubber floor mats duct-taped to the bench where a lifter would rest his back. AC began pressing weights while at the same time continuing his chat with O'Connolly.

The man couldn't stay still—he was up swapping out one set of weights for another, then dropping to the floor to knock off a few quick pushups, followed by two lengthy planks. Then rapidly back on his feet, still talking while placing additional weights on the two-inch bar resting above the bench.

"Stuff you see in the movies with Shwarzenegger and Stallone? That's Hollywood bullshit. You *really* wanna take down a building, you better know what you're doing," AC said.

There was a noise burst from a ringtone close by. It sounded like tanks or heavy equipment moving. O'Connolly watched the young man reach into a faded-green canvas bag and pull out a smartphone. Looking at the phone for a beat, he tapped the screen and held the phone out directly in front of his mouth.

"Kiss . . . my . . . ass," he yelled, put the phone back into the bag and lowered himself to the bench. He gripped the weight bar above him, took a deep breath and began pressing again.

A-D-H-D, O'Connolly thought. He wondered who'd been on the other end of the phone.

After five quick thrusts, AC placed the bar back in the slots above his head and got up from the bench.

How much weight's on that bar? O'Connolly didn't ask the question and AC wasn't even breaking a sweat.

11

PAY ATTENTION

"Let's take a little walk," AC said, pointing to the steel door of his seaworthy abode. O'Connolly wasn't sure. Walking was not his favorite mode of transportation. He was more of a lean back, stretch out and put your legs up kinda guy. "C'mon. I'll show you something. Give you an idea of what you're up against."

AC was already through the door. O'Connolly turned and followed, thinking about how he'd connected with this jamoke via Tommy Mac. *Truth is,* O'Connolly thought, *I might be the real jamoke here.* AC seemed pretty well on top of things.

Two minutes later, standing between parked cars and a double pen of shopping carts, AC was pointing back at the huge Wunder Mart main building.

"So *that* is a 180,000-square-foot structure." Taking a step back, he added, "You see why they call em 'big box' huh?"

O'Connolly was looking at AC but shifted his gaze to take in the super store. It was fucking *huge.* He nodded.

"Yeah?"

"If some dickhead was gonna try to blow this place, no brainer. All one level, high ceiling. Steel frame, wood, bricks and cement. Place the explosives, depending on what he used, in maybe six places. But they gotta be the *right* places."

AC looked at O'Connolly to be sure the dude was paying attention. His mouth was slightly agape, and he wasn't saying anything, so he must be listening.

"Down in Australia, back in the '90s, they tried to blow up a hospital and screwed the pooch. Big chunks of cement and steel blew more than 500 yards. Killed a little girl and injured a bunch of spectators," AC said. He paused and made eye contact with O'Connolly.

"You find the primary vertical supports, then place the explosives *selectively.* Big help if you could get hold of the blueprints." Turning to look at the building again like a tour guide pointing out hard-to-detect marks on ancient ruins, he continued his spiel.

"Once the explosives are ready, the key is to determine the sequence of detonation. It's not all one big, loud bang. That fucking just won't do it, dude. Know what I'm saying?"

O'Connolly didn't respond.

AC went on with his little parking lot seminar. "Then you wanna be particular in what you use. And how much. Bunch of jobs when some yahoo discovered a 'failure threshold' when they didn't use enough explosives. And it *didn't fucking work."*

Finally, O'Connolly got to the point, interrupting AC's monologue.

"I have, let's call him 'an acquaintance,' who has a little project in mind. Needs a pro to handle it. Tommy Mac says you can help."

AC studied the man. *Who the fuck is this guy?*

With a quick jerk of his head, AC went silent. He motioned again for O'Connolly to follow him, leading him back inside the steel container.

Let's hear what horseshit plan he has in mind.

"Okay, dude. Tell me *all* of it. Don't jerk my chain and leave anything out," AC said, straddling the weight bench and lowering himself slowly.

O'Connolly looked around. He sat in the taped-up plastic chair and said: "It's a little fucked up. But it could work. Might be best if I have you meet my acquaintance first."

12

TALENT AND SKILL

"Bffffff...." said the barefoot man in swim trunks, creating the playful mouth sound for another launch out across the white stretch of sand.

The missile was a multi-colored, waterproof beach football.

Running barefoot near 15 yards in the opposite direction to catch the ball was his nine-year-old son. And the kid *pulled it in* before his feet touched the surf. He looked back and dad gave him a big fist pump.

Two months after the last post-season game, one might think this quarterback would give it a rest. Not a chance.

He threw some kind of football—leather, nerf, hydro—nearly every day of the year. It was one of the many reasons why he was so much better than any other currently active play caller.

Tyler "Biff" Bradley, six-three and 215 pounds, exemplified the "10,000 hours" theory of developing skills and competence. He'd been playing football at some level since he was four years old. Now 41, you could think that he was still playing college. And that's where the *Bffff* routine got started. He did it so often in practice that teammates tagged him with the nickname. Today, naysayers and armchair critics, not to mention a few whining football fans around the country, frequently used the nickname as a term of derision.

"The Biffer," as some close friends called him, would simply offer up a smile. It was his eyes that conveyed: Yeah? Let's see *your* pass. But he never articulated those words. He just went out and played the game. Year after year after year. At a sustained level of excellence few had ever seen.

Aside from the usual demands of conditioning, nutrition and maintaining his trademark optimism, even when he didn't bring home another MVP trophy, he had a new challenge: convincing his wife that he was capable of "a few more years."

Conversations over the past 36 months had frequently included the observation: "You've been really lucky. Why push it? Walk away now."

Gabriella Sophia Bonita, the wife—wildly successful fashion model, clothing designer and a former Miss

Universe—was not unfamiliar with ambition, competitiveness and the overpowering desire to do things perfectly. But, like so many who'd never played professional sports, she really could not fully grasp what the game meant to a person on the fence about retirement.

Actually, he really wasn't on the fence at all. He just walked by the concept now and then. It was everyone *else* who endlessly yammered on about it. Sportswriters, radio and TV talking heads, fans, cab drivers, players from other teams, Jesuit priests reading the sports section of their hometown newspaper, tarot card readers. No shortage of speculation out there.

Meanwhile, back to the sand and surf: another missile launched too far over the kid's outstretched arms. He misses it. The ball lands with a splash. "Pik-kooool," the mouth sound for the missile hitting the water. Biff throws his arms skyward, shakes his head and laughs.

The kid fetches the ball from the water. After a quick arm motion for his son to come back up the beach, Biff does a couple of short sprints on the sand, followed by a spin, set and throw maneuver with an imaginary ball.

Only three months until summer training camp.

13

USA LADIES

Trooper Julie Egan could do squats, planks, kettlebell swings, hip raises, reverse lunges and practically any other exercise routine known to woman or man. What she liked most was spinning.

Headphones on, pedals and seat adjusted, water bottle in its holder, Julie began a cycling-in-place regimen and let her mind taxi toward lift off. The music mix: strictly '80s; *The Tide is High, Every Breath You Take, Material Girl* and more tracks to get her through the next 30 minutes.

Before the first drop of perspiration, she had a sudden inspiration:

Time to pay a visit to Jack the Cabbie, she thought, legs pumping and pedals on her exercise bike going full speed.

She had held off the visit, although she had been doing her research.

For one thing, she discovered that in Scotland he—or some rather eccentric American closely fitting the description—was known as the Fishing Bandit.

The Daily Telegraph

Grantown-on-Spey, Scotland—Gillies and riverkeepers here in the famous Highlands along this Bucolic green valley of grazing sheep, through which runs the storied River Spey, are looking for a thief. He is not the ordinary culprit, surreptitiously tapping into casks of whisky in smaller, un-guarded distilleries, but a lone angler who has every District Salmon Fishery Boards from Tweedside to Royal Deeside up in arms.

Sir Hugh Percival McDonough, a leading salmon fishing expert, holding forth at the Hare & Hound pub, told reporters that the "Fishing Bandit" is likely an American.

The illicit angler, explained Sir Hugh, fishes the best reaches of private water, called "beats," in the morning before the rightful anglers have finished their bangers-and-fried-egg breakfasts. He then vanishes, having spoiled the chances for the anglers, who are paying sometimes more than £10.000 for a week of sport. Sometimes the shadowy visitor reappears when the anglers have reeled in for their afternoon tea-and-whisky break, taking advantage of the inebriated fishing party, typically sprawled and snoring on the bank.

"He's nothing but a low-life robber, sneak, trespasser, a despicable poacher," the phlegmatic McDonough said, sipping the first of his afternoon gin and tonics. "He must be apprehended and sent packing this season!" pounding the palm of his hand on the dark wood table. His face was bright pink.

The lone angler apparently gains entry to these exclusive beats by using a variety of miniature watercraft, including portable folding canoes, tiny military sea rafts, even children's inflatable pool toys shaped like dragons and giraffes.

Tradition dictates that boats are not permitted on most Highland salmon rivers, and even then, only when rowed by a proper gillie.

"This reprobate is a disgrace. He's a villain! I tell you," Sir Hugh said loudly, adding that the Fishing Bandit violates every norm of traditional Scottish fishing etiquette and sanctity. "Scoundrel must be a Yank. They put ice in their whisky, you know."

Egan showered and suited up. She checked in at the barracks, answered messages, and at 10:07 a.m. drove north toward the Fox Bowl.

She scanned three parking lots before she spied the camo deer stand, on stilts. She drove across the lot slowly, tires crunching softly, and pulled up to the stand. Shutting the door quietly, she walked over and called up.

"Hello?"

A man in a Sherlock Holmes deerstalker tweed cap poked his head out. He was smoking an heirloom ivory Meerschaum pipe.

"Well, hello there," Jack said with a smile. "I've been expecting you sooner or later, young lady."

Julie climbed the thin ladder on one side and pulled herself into the hunting blind. She stood and extended her hand. "Julie Egan," she said. "New on the job."

"Jack," he answered and shook her hand. "Greetings and salutations!"

"I'm making myself an espresso," he motioned to the De'Longhi Dedica machine, steaming and whistling. "Please join me." His T-shirt with a leaping Atlantic salmon read GILLIE TO THE STARS. He motioned for her to sit in a movie director's chair that read, in stenciled letters, COPPOLA.

"You're probably wondering what in blazes I'm doing here in this deer stand in the middle of a parking lot."

"I wasn't supposed to ask," Julie said.

"You didn't," Jack the Cabbie said. "And that's most gracious of you. Therefore, I'll tell you."

Jack recounted his long, happy, reasonably hassle-free life of driving a taxicab around Boston. "Then that rogue rideshare operation reared its ugly head," he said. "Now everyone with a shitbox on wheels thinks he's a professional cabbie."

"Just like half the idiots camped out in a Starbucks with a laptop think they're the next F. Scott Fucking Fitzgerald, or J.K. Rowling," Egan said.

Jack puffed on his pipe and sipped the espresso. *Umm, this kid's all right.*

"So, started seriously thinking about hanging it up—maybe retiring to Bigfoot, Idaho. And then one day I picked up the phone. It was this loud Russian guy. I'd heard of him. Word had it that he was running some kind of dodgy taxi service for horny teenage boys. I know—sounds crazy . . . ."

Julie stopped him. "Jack, due respect, I think I know the story: the Marilyn Monroe lookalikes and all that. Were you involved?"

"Not in the beginning," Jack said. "Chump change and really not my thing. But the Russian character told me he wanted to up the game. He asked around and kept hearing that if anyone had any creative ideas, that would be me."

Julie said, "That must have been flattering."

"I don't know about that, but this Dimitri invited me to Fenway for a hot dog and a beer. Had season tickets, third base line. Between innings I listened carefully to what the guy had to say. Next week I got back to him with a plan."

Jack said that the idea was simple: to rake in more cash per "Meet the President" taxi ride—a lot more.

"I figured we already got Marilyn. Let's add Jackie. And while we're at it, Gloria Swanson, too."

For 25 grand, Jack explained, from one to a maximum of three customers would get picked up at Logan in a 1962 red Cadillac convertible, completely restored. Jack had the connections to get on to the tarmac, where the private jets come in. In his trademark flourish, he described showing up dressed in a period chauffeur's uniform, complete with bow tie and a little narrow-brim cap. When the door to the plane opened and the VIP customers walked down the stairs, they heard *Hail to the Chief* blasting from a magnetic megaphone on the roof. They walked on a red carpet to the Caddy where the girls were waiting.

"We pulled this off pretty nicely for maybe six months or so," Jack said. "Until three Chinese businessmen showed up. Flew in from New York, from Teterboro. They had a case of Scotch with them. Good stuff. Nothing under 18. By the time we get to the Sagamore Bridge over the canal these jokers are shitfaced."

Jack told Trooper Egan to imagine the picture-perfect Marylin, Jackie and Gloria babes sitting on the laps on these three Chinese guys, petting their cheeks softly and whispering in their ears. Jack said he glanced to his right at the passenger seat and then looked in the rearview mirror to the backseat and asked if they were enjoying themselves: "You gentlemen having a good time?" All had goofy smiles.

One of the men raised his glass to Jack and said, in reasonably fair English but with a distinct accent, "USA ladies hot!" It sounded like something between way-dees and ray-dees. Jack paused, looking out at the parking lot. "You're too young to know who Ray Deez was—promising lefty had one season with the Sox. Got injured, got traded, then got out of baseball altogether. Anyway. . . .

Back to our Hyannis misadventure," Jack continued. He told Julie that the Asian businessman pal next to him in back spouted, "USA ladies hot, hot, *hot!*"

And then the guy in the passenger seat chimed in with the other two and in unison the threesome proclaimed, "USA ladies *hot to trot!*" One of them passed out in Gloria Swanson's lap.

He delivered them to the rented cottage in Hyannis, tribal home of the Kennedy clan, and got the guests settled. Jack had sweet-talked the Russian to pay for painted wicker furniture and walls covered with late 1950s and early '60s framed movie posters. When Jack switched on the lights, automatically the theme from *A Summer Place* began playing, the strings of Percy Faith and his orchestra animating the balmy Cape Cod September night.

"I told them to take a hot-tub with the girls—a chef would be by soon with lobsters, Jack said. "I figured they'd be kept busy between the booze and the broads, the old Sinatra playbook." No such luck.

"I'm on the beach, glassing the Vineyard Sound for busting bluefish at dusk," Jack went on. "I see flashing blue lights go by. I race back to the cottage. The girls said the Chinese guys had called a self-driving piece-of-junk electric skateboard of a car and taken off somewhere. *Oh shit*, I remember thinking."

What Jack hadn't realized is that the foreign visitors had a portable ladder stashed in their duffel, a kind of rock-climbing device. They tossed it over the wall at the actual Kennedy Compound down 6A in Hyannisport. They were busy hoisting themselves and what was left of the case of Scotch up and over when the Barnstable County sheriff appears on the scene and hauls the drunken Chinamen off to jail.

"I escaped with the girls," Jack said, "but it didn't take the cops long to find the Russian. The state attorney general's office decided that I was a relatively harmless accomplice and gave me a plea-bargain. Your fellow state cops kindly assigned me to keep an eye on comings and goings here at Fox Bowl. They had been intercepting some suspicious chatter on social media."

"Are the Pirates paying you?" Egan asked.

"Not a penny. Let's just say I'm doing sentry duty as kind of an act of contrition for all us fallen Catholics."

Jack paused. "You're also probably too young to know about Gloria Swanson."

"Mr. DeMille, I'm ready for my closeup," Julie said, exaggerated eyes wide open and chin thrust forward. "Possessor of one of the great cinematic endings of all time in Billy Wilder's *Sunset Boulevard*? And old man Joe Kennedy's silent-screen mistress in the twenties? *That* Gloria Swanson?"

"Bravo! Bravo!" said Jack the Cabbie, clapping lightly and puffing his vintage Meerschaum with the yellowing patina.

14

TEN PERCENT

A **Hail Mary pass** short of the Golden Triangle, just 20 yards from the north bank of the Allegheny River, in the city of Pittsburgh, commonwealth of Pennsylvania—home of the *baseball* Pirates—another former professional football player had some time on his hands.

Mooko Deganawida, aka Marshall Deegan, looked at his phone vibrating on the table in front of him. The phone was shimmying its way to the edge and would likely fall to the tiled floor on the next *zzzztt*.

With the huge, strong hand of a "coulda been" All-Pro tight end, Mooko reached for the phone. It continued vibrating as he studied the screen. *Incoming Call—617.466.3337.*

"This Mooko. Who you?" he said into the phone.

"Mook. I'm putting together a travel squad. Gonna go up and play some of those tough fucking Indians in Canada this summer. Some of your people. Need a guy who can run almost as fast as I can."

Mooko knew the voice, recognized the wiseass tone.

"LaChance, you run 'bout as fast as a sorry ass bayou turtle with blisters on his feet."

"But a *handsome* turtle," Whitey said. "And with great hands."

The retort caused Mooko to smile. He looked at his lady friend and held up a right index finger as he stood from the table at the outdoor café

Now six-seven, 275 pounds, Mooko had been a tall, skinny roommate and teammate with Whitey in college. Known then only by the name Marshall Deegan, during a confusing period of his young life, he'd later walked away from the game just a year after being drafted high and signed low, as in "minimum salary" low.

These days, using the name that he claimed had come from his Iroquois Nation ancestors, Mooko was, by his own definition, a "glorified security gofer and community liaison" employed by a Pittsburgh real estate development company.

Aside from his professional duties, he really liked to gamble. On anything, from major sports betting to back room penny ante games run by a construction pal. One of the reasons Mooko liked gambling was because he won more often than he lost. Just a lucky guy. And he didn't piss away his winnings, always on the lookout for entertaining new ways to rake in more chips.

Back to the phone call, at Mooko's end: "What's up, bro? Don't be tellin me you actually gonna *play* somewhere! Lemme guess—you got a bunch of pilgrim crackers all lined up to sponsor a celebrity golf event over der in Massy'chusetts?"

"Nah, man. I eat so many doughnuts, fucking high school kids would kick my butt."

"Come down here. I'll show you a little CrossFit get you back in shape in two weeks," Mooko said.

"Maybe. But I got a project gonna keep me busy for a while. That's why I'm callin. I could use your help. What're the chances, man, you can come to Boston?"

"When?"

"Sooner is good. Like this weekend," Whitey said.

"You want to tell me about it?"

"Not on the phone, kinda delicate situation. I'd sure love some help. And this ain't no freebie. You get some cash when we're done."

It took only another minute for Mooko and Whitey to agree that they could meet in two days, somewhere near Boston. Not a fan of flying, unless absolutely necessary, Mooko said that he would drive up and would let Whitey know his ETA.

Whitey was confident that once he made his pitch on the Fox Bowl Project that Mooko would sign on.

The primary factor boosting Whitey's confidence was the most recent calibration in his relationship with Shauntay.

Following a lukewarm spell that had quickly gone cold after one of their frequent fights, they were back to "hot" again. So hot that Whitey was not worrying, for the moment, anyway, about Shauntay's spending habits and his subsequent credit card statements.

Only hours before his call to Mooko, in a display of both her dominatrix skills and her tenderness, Shauntay had assured Whitey that she thought that she could get some funds to underwrite his plan.

"But, baby, you *do* have to have a plan. No foolin around here," she said. "You comin up with something big, it has to work. When you're ready, you tell me all about it and we go from there." She kissed him, then climbed out of bed to get ready for another shopping jaunt.

Whitey *knew* that Shauntay *knew* some people. She had her own circle, connections to women who spent more than she did on lots of things—clothes, travel, jewelry. He was beginning to imagine a way past the "big bucks" stumbling block placed in front of him by The Mayor: "I connect you with the guy who can pull this together, before it's all done, it could cost a million. Maybe more." And AC Cahill had conveyed as much.

The figure had temporarily put the brakes on Whitey's wild-ass, half-baked idea of "slowing the income stream" of the people who had treated him poorly.

Following several days of fantasizing, he'd found the archived TV documentary and watched it again. Whitey could see large sections of a stadium imploding before his very eyes.

From the very first thought, he had no desire to cause bodily injury to anyone. His imagination had come up with a scenario of "BOOM in the middle of the night." That could work.

Then let the fuckers see how many concerts, soccer matches, football games, religious revivals and monster truck rallies kept the cash flowing. Christ, half the fucking country hates the Pirates anyway. Least half.

Jasmine gave him her best toy breed smile and a little panting.

"Munchies tomorrow, *baby*," he exaggerated, scratching the little dog's ears.

Following their first meeting, O'Connolly had concluded that if he really had been the mayor of Somerville, or any fucking city, that he would put AC Cahill in charge of public works. Maybe the planning division, too.

Now he was heading back to Walpole and a follow-up rendezvous, this time in the garden and outdoors pavilion of the Super Wunder Mart. AC had told him that it was a good place to "clear your head." *Okay. Will do. Ten-four.*

And there he was. Camo cargo shorts, a faded green fatigue T-shirt that looked one size too small and flip-flops. But it was the sunglasses that made him stand out: reflective fluorescent blue mirror lenses in a bright white plastic frame studded with red diamond shapes on the temples.

When AC spotted The Mayor coming in his direction, he dropped to the floor and did five quick one-hand push-ups. He stood, rotated his neck slowly and motioned for O'Connolly to join him next to the patio furniture section. Pulling out one of the fake wicker chairs, AC sat and put his feet up on a table. O'Connolly took a matching chair and sat across from him.

"What's the story, Mayor?" AC asked.

O'Connolly looked around to see if anyone was close enough to hear them. Nope. Shifting his ass to get comfortable, but not putting his feet up, he folded his arms and rested them on the glass table. And said nothing.

AC extended his arms out as though he were inveighing the masses to join him in song, or perhaps doing an imitation of Keith Lockart about to lead the Boston Pops at Tanglewood.

"We got a deal or not?" AC asked.

O'Connolly cleared his throat, uncrossed his arms, then refolded them. After another quick glance over his shoulder, he leaned in closer.

"I think the next step is you meet this guy. One on one. No reason for me to be there," he said, watching for a reaction.

AC had taken his feet down, sat forward, curled both hands under his chin and rested his elbows on the table. He pursed his lips in silence.

The Mayor could see his own reflection in the sunglasses. Twice.

"You fellows like each other, put together a deal, great. I take a small referral fee. It doesn't look like it'll work, you tell this bozo to fuck off and go pound sand," O'Connolly said.

AC offered the slightest smile. He lowered his hands and placed them flat on the glass patio table—on sale this week for just $149, including four chairs.

"Two things," AC said. "One, how much is a 'small' referral fee?"

"Ten percent," O'Connolly said.

"Not including supplies," AC said.

"Sure."

"And second," AC said, reaching across the table and tightly gripping O'Connolly's left forearm, "let me assure you, dude, I know something about pounding sand. So, save that kinda' pseudo tough talk for your pals in fucking Dorchester or wherever."

The Super Wunder Mart meeting of the minds ended relatively well. Or, at least as well as The Mayor could have hoped for, considering that he was on both ends of a possible deal with two of the craziest, most potentially dangerous clowns he'd ever come across.

Fifty-grand. That was the "fee" O'Connolly had calculated to get this show on the road. It would be up front, thank you, Mister "*fooot*-bawl-air." If and when he had a sense that something was actually *happening*, The Mayor would step back in for an accounting of the project's costs. Maybe another cash installment would be appropriate.

Back in his room at The Hilltop Motel, O'Connolly prepared to call Whitey to tell him the next play. Cash, call, go. Let me know what else I can do. And good fucking luck.

15

CRAB FRITTERS

"It's been brought to my attention," the announcer said, "that we're getting calls from all over the country. Bunch of football crazies with nothing else to do, huh?"

For this evening's show, he was using the on-air name of Fran Tarkenton.

"Well, isn't that just ducky? The internet, streaming audio, delayed programming. Hooray for us." The sound effect of a large crowd cheering.

"One of my associates here at Radio-Free Beanville, has suggested that we also consider a podcast. To which *I say* . . . two pees in a pod . . . makes a full urinal." An exaggerated groan sound effect and the crowd booing.

"Okay, that was not up to our usual standards. Could be because the 'associate' who made the suggestion is only five-two. But I told him that this is what we will do. Tonight, and tonight *only*, we shall give priority to *all calls* coming from anywhere outside the 27,337 kilometers squared that comprise the Commonwealth of Massachusetts." Cheering crowd encore.

"It's on your nickel, friend: *617—two-five, two-five*."

The canned intro, reverb announcer and all, played over the theme from *Chariots of Fire*. After the horns building and a long stretch of a synthesizer, followed by the salutary piano chord, Fran was back: "Now the Forecast."

"And remember, *football*. Don't be calling to talk about a bunch of guys running barefoot on the beach. That won't do, mate. We're all about *American* football. Got it?" The music played on for another 30 seconds before Fran took his first call.

"Hello in . . . Edgewater, Maryland. You're on the radio."

"Hey, Fran. How's it goin?"

"Goin fine, thank you. How's the softshell crab season down there in Mary-Land?"

"Great. Wife fixed up some fritters this morning. A cold beer. Sweet."

Fran: "You drink beer in the *morning*?"

Caller: "Not every morning. Special occasions. Gotta be in the mood, if you know what I mean."

Fran: "Okay. That works, I guess. What beer does one drink with the crab fritters . . . ahem, in the morning?"

Caller: "Yeungling Traditional Lager."

More yuk, yuk about craft beers, Chesapeake Bay blue crab versus New England lobster, then eventually on to the caller's main point: undrafted college football players, walk-ons.

"Are there any statistics on how many of these guys actually make it with a team, I mean for the entire league?" the caller asked.

"I'm sure there are. So, you got 32 teams, what, 53 players on each roster? That doesn't count practice squads, so add five more, gets you to 58. Uh . . . let' see here." Fran made a sound imitating an adding machine for a few seconds, then offered: "1,856 players total. At any given point during the season."

"With players being let go all the time, right?" the caller added. "And that's another factor. So, my neighbor's son, he's got it in his head that he wants to play professional football, even though he's spent virtually his entire college career on the bench at Towson. I think, maybe, he played in *two* games."

Silence from Fran. No music, no sound effects.

"And . . . *and*, get this," the caller went on, "the kid's maybe five-six on a good day, 160 pounds tops."

More silence, then Fran replied: "Okay. Here's what you need to do. Invite this young man over for, say, crab fritters and a beer."

"Sure, I can do that."

"Ask him to *pay close attention* to what you're about to tell him."

"Yeah?" the caller said.

"Be nice, tactful right? Let him eat the fritters."

"Okay."

"Make good eye contact, speak slowly. And then tell Mister 'Five-Six, Hundred-and-Sixty Pounds' the following: 'Son, there is a real shortage of Railroad Engineers in this country. Finish your beer and get on board'."

Click. The caller from Maryland was gone.

Fran: "On the radio from . . . Bowdoinham, Maine. Hey, what's up?"

"Thanks for taking my call. Big fan," the new caller said.

"You know what Groucho Marx said? On a day like today, I could *use* a big fan." Crowd cheering.

"So, what's on your mind this fine evening?"

Caller: "The Pirates first regular season game is just a few weeks from now. I haven't heard you make any season predictions yet. How's it lookin' to you?"

Fran: "It seems to me, and I've also given this a *lot* of thought, that . . . Coach Willy, no doubt, will have *squinted* through 50-plus hours of regular season action. Do the math—average game is three hours and 12 minutes."

Caller: "Sure. But a lot of that time, nothin's *happening.* Players just standing around or are running on and off the field. The clock's still going."

Fran: "Yes, that's how the game is played here in America. Somebody once calculated that if we just measure the time that the ball is actually *in play*, it comes to . . . wait, I've got it here somewhere." The theme from *Dragnet* came up for six seconds.

"Eleven minutes," Fran blurted out. "Shorter than any church service that I know about. Here it is again: *11 . . . minutes.* The time that the ball is in play. Average of something like four-and-a-half seconds for each play, maybe 140 plays total."

Caller: "Wow. That's unbelievable. So, what's your prediction?"

Fran: "Think about it. They figured out a few years ago that a televised game spends more time, like *18 minutes*, showing reviews of plays, compared to the 11 minutes when the ball is moving."

Caller: "So, this season. Whad'ya predicting?"

Fran: "That it will end sooner than you can miss a field goal. You want *predictions*? Call one of the other shows. Those two guys in the morning and their pals? I think they do predictions."

Click. Bowdoinham caller sent to the showers.

Following a five-minute, way-too-much-information monologue on the real New England weather forecast for the next week, including two bad puns and one very old joke, and after insulting two additional out-of-state callers, the show was wrapping up.

"Back here on Monday night. For those who still wear leather helmets, your host w*ill be Johnny Unitas.*" It was the Looney Tunes theme music ending this show.

"And for young men contemplating a career in professional football, study up on the kid who Notre Dame *would not accept* because he was too . . skinny! *And* . . . who was released by the Pittsburgh Steelers before his first season." Music up for :08 seconds, ending with Porky Pig's "That's All Folks."

16

BIRD SHIT

The Corvette circled the Wunder Mart lot slowly. Whitey braked, backed up, sat with the engine idling for a full minute before he figured out that the shipping container was located behind the main store.

Maybe the Mayor had told him that, but then he'd told him so much that somehow that part didn't register.

Glancing left, then right, to see if anyone was watching, Whitey did a half-turn and drove to the far end of the lot. He parked, got out of the car and walked toward the shipping containers. There were five of them. One stood out: it was a bright orange, the color, he thought in passing, of the Clemson football uniforms.

Stopping a couple feet short of the container, Whitey listened.

"Now I want you to remember, that no bastard *ever* won a war. . . . " It was a recording, a soundtrack from a movie. Sounded familiar. He was sure that he'd heard it but couldn't think who it was. The volume inside the shipping container was loud enough that you could feel the vibration.

Whitey got closer and rapped on the door, two loud knocks. Nothing. The guy in the movie continued his lecture.

"He won it, by making the *other* poor dumb bastard. . . ."

Whitey knocked again. The door jerked open and he was looking at maybe Arnold Schwarzenegger's skinny younger brother, but bald with a buzz cut, like he'd just been bused out of boot camp.

Whitey took a step back. The guy pushed the door open. Behind him, on a big screen TV, Whitey could see a huge American flag. There was a soldier with a bunch of medals wearing a helmet. He was the one in the movie giving a speech. With the door open, the speakers really were vibrating. The man hit a button on a remote device in his left hand and the sound went mute.

"You're the 'acquaintance' The Mayor sent over," the man said.

Whitey nodded, then stuck out his right hand. The man turned his back without shaking hands.

"C'mon in," the man said.

Whitey couldn't take his eyes off the movie playing on the giant flat screen. Some World War II general or something. *What the fuck was his name?*

"Let's not waste a lot of time here, friend," the man went on, still with his back to Whitey. "The Mayor says you've got a big project. You need a demolitions expert. Is that right?"

Now the man turned to face Whitey. Wearing a faded gray T-shirt that perhaps had been in the dryer one cycle too long, or, was a smaller size to begin with, contrasting with bright, floral pattern beach shorts and a pair of flip-flops. Not really Schwarzenegger's brother, more like one of those young Olympic weightlifters. Maybe one of the pro wrestler types from TV. *John what's-his-name?*

The man stared at Whitey, who was still somewhat distracted by the army officer up on the big screen, talking but no sound coming out of the speakers. The American flag behind the soldier was the size of a house.

Tapping a button on the remote, the man killed the video and the big screen went blank. He threw the remote onto an army cot off to the side next to a weight bench.

"Have a seat," the man said, gesturing to a plastic chair. "Let's hear your story."

Ten minutes after he'd arrived, Whitey had finished stammering his way through a shaky idea about blowing up a "facility" not far from where they sat. Only when the man pressed him did he fess up that he was talking about a football stadium.

"Dude, are you fucking *kidding me?*" the man said. He stared at Whitey in disbelief.

Rising from the plastic chair, Whitey held up both hands in resignation. He shook his head, smiled and turned toward the door.

"Yeah. I'm kidding," Whitey said. "Thought maybe a guy like you, war veteran and all, would know how to get a tractor trailer filled with TNT inside without no one being the wiser. Then: Ba-da-BOOM! Impossible, right? Sorry I bothered you."

Long silence.

"Hold on," the younger man said. "Set back down. Let me tell you why your idea is *bullshit.* And then I'll tell you what *might* work."

Whitey took his seat again. Spellbound, he listened to this weightlifting, buzz cut, detail-oriented deadbeat succinctly rip apart his idea as being lame and simplistic, followed by, as far as Whitey could tell, a totally improvised plan to accomplish what Whitey had really wanted since he'd first seen the Rolling Stones poster and then watched the documentary about blowing up buildings.

"Three things, dude," the man said. "Timing, grunts, cash. One, something this big, takes time. You don't fucking drive by and throw a coupla sticks of dynamite—or drive a damn truck in and leave it running." He was shaking his head.

"Two, it's like going into battle. You gotta have support. Probably five guys besides me, maybe four if they're good."

And, he added—the biggie—"you better have more fucking money than you got with your signing bonus back in the day."

It was in that second that Antoine LeBlanc, Junior, aka the Bayou Flash, aka Whitey or Boom-Boom, realized that this joker knew who he was.

Sharing a pint of Ben & Jerry's Cherry Garcia, passing the container back and forth like it was a pint of whisky, AC Cahill and Whitey reached tentative agreement on a plan.

It would start with AC doing some reconnaissance and photography of the Fox Bowl. Once he'd completed that, they would settle on a timeline, likely materials and a first-round cost estimate.

Standing at the open door of the shipping container, Whitey pulled a roll of cash from his pocket. AC watched him peeling off bills.

"Ten-grand get us started?" Whitey asked.

"Barely," AC said, taking the money. "Bring 50 next time. If we go beyond that, better get a line of credit or rob a bank."

Whitey fumbled the few remaining bills back into his pocket. He'd already given The Mayor 25 big ones just to connect him with this "expert."

AC, flexing his shoulders and pecs as though he was about to lift weights, gave a big smile. "You know what the asking price is on a Porsche 918 Spyder?" he asked.

Whitey shrugged. "Two-fifty, 300?"

AC jerked both thumbs up a couple times.

"Half a million?"

"Eight-fifty. That was last winter," AC said. "This project of yours, that's the kind of money we're talkin about." AC turned away to go back inside his bunker. Over the shoulder, now flexing his neck and rotating his arms, he added, "Better tell me now if that scares you, dude. Let's not be wasting time."

No reply from Whitey. Moving weights around on the floor, AC heard the door close behind him.

Shuffling back to the car, Whitey thought about the money. Again. Fifteen years earlier, the signing bonus had been what he thought of at the time as a cool million. That was chickenfeed now. Three teams later, along with one piddly endorsement deal, unstable relationships with a few women, and now the never-ending demands of Shauntay, it all added up to a lot of cash being pumped into the economy.

Sitting in his car and staring back at the shipping container with the big Aquaman seal on the door, Whitey tried to bring up an image of a Porsche 918 Spyder.

Guess we know what motivates that white boy.

Two hours later, speed-walking the perimeter of the Wunder Mart parking lot, earbuds from his iPhone firmly in place, AC tapped in the number for The Mayor.

"An eagle just shit on my roof and we're under way," AC said.

"Was the eagle driving a yellow Corvette?" The Mayor asked.

"Fuck if I know. He left already. We're going soaring again next week. I'll let you know how it goes."

"I am *so* pleased that you birders could spend some time together."

The Mayor put his phone down and brought the TV volume up. Hannity was haranguing about something from the Southern District of New York, Rudy Giuliani and people in D.C. Then the screen showed the image of an odd-looking older white male with ashen face, charcoal iris and pupils topped with burgundy eyebrows and dyed blonde hair.

"Ah, Sean, me lad," O'Connolly said aloud, conjuring his dear late grandfather's fondly reverberating Irish brogue.

"I'm afraid more a yer fine boys will be takin' time off from life for a wee spell behind the bars."

Hannity didn't appear to be fazed by this revelation.

17

WHUMP

Walking in the afternoon sun on Newbury Street, keeping a tight leash on Jasmine, Shauntay prattled on about plans for a small party for a few close women friends.

Whitey was half listening, distracted by the magnificent sight of two young women on the sidewalk just ahead. What *really* distracted him was their swaying rear ends. Designer jeans, indeed. "Derrière," he said, smiling. And thinking that he was talking to himself.

"*What?*" Shauntay asked tersely, pulling on his arm.

He stopped, hesitated, then foolishly repeated the word. "Derrière. It means. . . ."

"I *know* what it means."

Shuantay had also observed the two young women, now a little farther up the street. She and Whitey had stopped abruptly. Jasmine, stretching the retractable leash, turned to look back at Mama.

Whitey looked up at the sky, down at the sidewalk, out at cars going by, but he did not look at Shauntay. Jasmine gave a little yelp—Whitey looked at her.

"What is *wrong* with you," Shauntay said, wide-eyed with ram-rod straight posture right there for pedestrians to observe as they maneuvered around the face off.

Whitey held his hands up in surrender and tried a 'you caught me' smile. Bad move. Shauntay was seeing *no* humor in this latest incident of her man "just lookin." Reeling in the leash and bending forward, Shauntay scooped Jasmine into her arms and was off at an accelerated pace, heels clicking on the sidewalk.

"Hey, baby. *Come on*," Whitey said. Waiting a couple of seconds, he glanced around to see how many others were watching. An older man seated on a bench was smiling at him. Whitey shrugged, shook his head and started after Shauntay. The two young women were long out of sight.

Black marble eyes, white coat, Jasmine sat at attention next to the closed bathroom door. A designer green and gold tote bag, embroidered with Shauntay's name, rested across the room on the sofa next to the retractable leash.

Whitey closed the door to the condo behind him and went to sit in a leather stressless chair, lifting his feet up onto the matching ottoman. He waited for Shauntay to reappear. After coming out of the bathroom five minutes later, she stood, arms folded, glaring at him and saying nothing. He knew the look and knew to tiptoe carefully. Jasmine bounced and circled for a minute before wisely going off to the kitchen.

"Baby, I'm sorry. I got a lot on my mind. I didn't mean to upset you," he said. "You know when I'm lookin at young girls' butts, it don't mean nothin."

No verbal response. Possibly an uptick on the *I'll-strangle-you* meter.

"Come on, honest, baby," he repeated. "Don't mean *nothin!*"

Pop. Meter just spiked. Shauntay unfolded her arms, took a step toward Whitey, stopped and, with more force than really necessary, sat on the sofa next to the tote bag directly across from him. She refolded her arms.

"What I know, *Antoine* . . . is that when you checkin out every sweet little ass that crosses the street, you are *not* thinking about me," Shauntay said. She repeated "*me*" and tapped her breastbone.

The Whites'ter kept his mouth shut. Good time to listen.

Shauntay leaned forward on the sofa, simultaneously reaching for the dog leash and placing the molded plastic case on her right thigh. She softly patted the case. Her other hand repeatedly snapped the clip end of the leash in and out of the case.

Jasmine came scampering back to the living room and jumped up next to Shauntay.

"No, baby, we've been for a walk. Later," Shauntay said, scratching the top of the dog's head and leaning over to give her a kiss. In the flick of an eyelash, like a corner back out of nowhere, Shauntay stood and hurled the dog leash at Whitey. His hands reflexed, but not quickly enough. The plastic case, the size of a bagel with a handle, but with the consistency of a hockey puck, hit him dead center in a slap shot to the crotch. Good aim.

Whitey howled.

Jasmine jumped down and gave two squeaky barks. Standing over him, Shauntay offered an additional observation.

"And what else I *know*," she exaggerated, "is that when you admiring . . . *derrières*, you not thinkin with your brain."

Both hands now protecting his package, Whitey squirmed to find a comfortable position. Other than a deep, slow groan, he retained the good sense not to say a word. Shauntay remained hovering. Jasmine offered another squeak bark, provoking Mama to give her the STOP gesture. And no more kisses.

"How long we been together?" Shauntay demanded. Hands on her hips and moving a couple of steps backward, while Jasmine leapt back to the sofa and sat a short distance away from Whitey, placing her in the neutral zone. The room went dead silent. No reply to Shauntay's question.

She pivoted, walked to the window looking out on the faux gaslights along the brick sidewalks, folded her arms and kept her back to Whitey and Jasmine. The sound of passing cars was barely audible. After a long 15 seconds, coulda been 15 *minutes*, Shauntay spoke again, voice restrained and barely above a forceful whisper.

"A lot on your mind?" she said. "I think you used that line when you came back from Louisiana. But when I asked you at the restaurant the other night, you said that you are 'thinking on a plan.' Am I *right*?" She turned to look at Whitey. "Still don't know *what* plan," she tacked on.

Not ready to respond, he pulled both feet up onto the ottoman, knees bent and he leaned forward. Maybe that helped the discomfort.

"Whatever you're planning best include paying more attention to me and *not* how long we been together, but just exactly what the *future* is looking like. You *hear* me?"

Whitey nodded, slowly lowered his legs and stood from the chair. He took a step toward Shauntay, but she now gave him the STOP signal.

"No," she said, right arm in a crossing guard position, hand up. "Antoine, you need to think about what you want, what you're doing with the rest of your life, and *who* you want to be with. You *understand* that?"

It was Whitey's turn to fold his arms as he looked away and remained silent. Jasmine turned around on the sofa a couple of times and made as though she might settle.

Shauntay walked past him returning to the bathroom. As she was closing the door, Whitey spoke up, "I can't stop thinking about the Fox Bowl. Gotta do something."

No response from Shauntay.

"Working an idea to slow-things-down there for this coming season." He leaned closer to the door. No water running, no flushing sounds. "It's gonna take a shitload of cash to get the plan off the ground," he added.

Still nothing from Shauntay. He looked back at Jasmine, curled into herself there on the sofa, one eye covered with a paw and the other looking at Whitey.

The bathroom door jerked open, Shauntay moved swiftly to the sofa, reached into the tote bag and pulled out a cardboard box the size of a small loaf of bread. With a pivot that Larry Bird would've admired, she passed Whitey again, smacking him on the side of the head with the box as she went by on her way to the bedroom. She slammed the door closed.

He was startled, but not hurt by the gratuitous dope slap. The box fell to the floor. Whitey picked it up and stared at it. There were the team colors and the logo above the brand name: The Official Tissue of the New England Pirates.

18

POP-POP

Shauntay knew her IQ score: 117. Whitey? Maybe 100, possibly a digit or two under. But what a body. Even with the increasingly soft paunch, Whitey was still her man, satisfying all of her wants and needs, not to mention that he also paid for her above-average lifestyle.

But there was a glitch: the ever-present concern that her man was going to fool himself into believing that he needed to have a quick roll in the end zone with some sweet young thing. If that happened, "Mama's coming, baby" would take on a whole new meaning.

With measured breathing, Shauntay adjusted the impact-sport electronic earmuffs, tapped a button inside the booth, extended her right arm to the proper position and placed her left hand to support the butt of the pistol. She waited for the paper targets to slide across 21 feet in front of her.

One hour once a week at the Mythic Ravine Gun Club, just minutes north of the city, was something Shauntay had locked onto her calendar, every Friday evening at 7. It was almost as good as sex. And Whitey had no idea of her new hobby.

The 14x24-inch silhouette moved left to right and popped up from the bottom randomly. With each target, she was able to get off all seven shots from her 9-millimeter Kahr PM9 ("Overall slim profile ideal for concealed carry!") featuring matte stainless-steel slide with night sights. It was lighter than a Glock and more expensive; she liked both qualities. And there was the patriotic aspect to consider—Shauntay's prized pistol was handcrafted in Worcester, at the state-of-the-art Kahr firearms factory on Goddard Drive.

Buy local, blast local. She thought it had a nice ring to it.

In a period of only six weeks at the range, using her superior eyesight and superb control, she could consistently score 100 percent on each target.

Another event locked onto the calendar immediately following her visits to the gun club was Friday night out with friends. A group of women who met for drinks and dinner at different restaurants around the city had become Shauntay's link to Life in Boston. While the size of the group varied, from three to six women depending on the week, it was always stimulating.

Look around at restaurant gatherings in nearly any town or city. If you see a group of men—or, in this case, women—there is some networking taking place. The group may be informal and may not have an official name, but more often than not, somebody's sharing information. Or offering a contact that can help with something.

Shauntay always listened. To the point that an objective observer might not recognize her as the same woman who kept "her man" in line. The same woman who also had ambition far exceeding her humble upbringing and life in rural North Carolina. Now she was in Boston, not the most racially welcoming metropolis in the Northeast. Before she left this city, she vowed to herself, people would know that Shauntay had been here.

On the radio: "Our main topic tonight . . . What's the story on Biff's number?" the host said, with the theme from the old TV program *Bonanza* playing for his intro.

"Hey, it's your old pal Dan Blocker here. Sul Ross State, 1950. Put your spikes on and give us a call."

With theme music under, up came heavy reverb for a voice that sounded like a cross between Porky Pig and a metro PA system. Complete with a fake stutter, listeners were treated to the show's pre-recorded opening.

"C-c-call today, folks. Operators are standing by." Still more reverb goosed the daily intro, "Now . . . *The Forecast.*"

"Six one seven—544-25-25," the host said. "Zager and Evans, 1969, for those who don't know. Look it up. 617-544-two-five, two-five."

The theme music faded and the host, formerly known as Bart Starr on the previous night's program, dramatically cleared his throat.

"Ack-hem. Let's see . . . ah, here it is! Right in front of me. Hot off the intertwining, *intercoursing*, and always entertaining friggin internet. Listen up. I have it right here some place." A horserace bugle call to post set up his announcement.

"Before I read this little gem, may I remind you; *football* . . . and the *weather.* That's it. Don't bring up insecure windbags disguised as elected members of the federal government. Don't whine about immigration laws, healthcare, the economy or any kind of 'peachments'. And *do not* try to slip in a personal greeting to your Aunt Millie in Malden.

"Football. Weather. That's it. Simple, right?

"Okay, where was I? Right. Let me read this. And bless this man.

In *Paw Paw*, West Virginia, not to be confused with *Pee Pee*, Ohio, there is a retired high school football coach who *pledges* to stand on a wooden soap box before every home game next fall. He *says* that he will wear a Roger Goodell

Clown T-shirt." The *Jaws* theme music comes in for the first of what possibly will be 10 times on tonight's show."

Otis "Bucky" Buckhannon, the host continued, "now 83 years old, says that *until* professional football, and specifically the *Commissioner*, accepts more responsibility in the ongoing development of athletes into role models and good citizens, *he*, that would be Coach Bucky there, will distribute pamphlets to parents, grandparents and anyone else within arm's reach, explaining *why* God created football. And what needs to be done to *save* the game."

Silence. No music, no sound effects.

"Okay, here's what we need to do," the host resumed. "Let's see if we can get Coach Bucky on the phone. It would be interesting to know *just how many* 'young athletes' from Paw Paw, West-by-God-Virginia have gone on to play professional football?"

More silence.

"If you have a thought or a brain fart that will help us out here, 617-544-two-five, two-five. Hello in Sudbury. You're on the radio."

"Yeah, Hoss. How ya' doin?" the caller said.

Before the man could say another word, the Bonanza theme came in again and the host pounced. "*Al-l-l* . . . right! Give this man tonight's plastic trophy." The theme galloped on for another five seconds.

"Bobby Dan Davis Blocker, 'Hoss' Cartwright to friends and family, was a *football* player *before* he was an actor. Look it up." The music faded and the host added, "So, what's on your mind, Sudbury?"

"Yeah. Could you explain, I know you talked about this the other night, could you tell me what you think is going on with the Players Association? How long're they going to put up with, as Tony Kornheiser said, the Commissioner hiding under his desk?"

"Good question."

For approximately three minutes, with no dead air, no music and *no* sound effects, the host sermonized on what *he* thought the players should do. He ended with one of his signature pieces about compensation.

"And while I, and all of the outstanding volunteers for this tiny, low-power signal of strength here at Radio Goal Post, work for *absolutely no remuneration*, not many players are gonna do much as long as they're getting a paycheck."

The oft-used theme from *Dragnet* came up for five seconds before the host went on.

"Course, you might *think* . . . that a few of the enlightened team owners . . . would dock the Commissioner's $35-million pay, huh? But *do not* bet the farm on that one, Bubba. In fact, don't be surprised if 'the Commish' gets a contract extension before the season starts. Thanks for your call.

And, uh, hello in . . . Sandwich. Make mine grilled cheese. You're on the radio."

There was a woman calling from the Cape to say only positive things about the Pirates and their amazing quarterback. The host, for a change, handled the caller with marginal politeness. He concluded with the observation that Biff's number will be retired at the beginning of the new season and that for the *rest of his active playing career*, he will be sporting just a large ***B*** on his jersey.

Then a man from Hartford, Connecticut weighed in via cellphone to grumble about ticket prices to *all* games, not just the pros. Still another guy piled on by calling to list every possible expense item associated with taking a family of four to a professional sporting event. When the caller made the mistake of referring to a recent outing at Fenway Park, the host gave him the hook and disconnected the call. A total of 14 calls made it on the air.

The *Bonanza* theme music came up and the show was ending. Over a stretch of one hour and 58 minutes, the host had controlled play for 66 percent of the game, callers got the other one-third. Both sides could have been called for multiple penalties, but there were no challenges.

"Be sure to show up for practice tomorrow night, kiddos," the host said. "Your host will be Sam Huff. Might want to wear a neck brace, could be a jarring experience. And maybe Sam can get us ol' Coach Bucky on the line."

When the theme music ended, the host was heard mumbling, "Anybody know where Little Joe is?"

19

FREE AGENT

It was a little after nine on a warm Friday evening when Mooko pulled into the parking lot of the Red Wing. He spotted the GO DEEP plates on Whitey's Corvette parked between a pickup and a pair of Harleys.

Once inside, he saw Whitey seated at a table near the back.

As Mooko walked toward him, Whitey threw a small blue and gold Tigers nerf football at him. Catching it in his left hand, Mooko quickly tapped the ball up in the air—it nearly hit a ceiling fan—then grabbed the ball with his right hand and held the catch above his head.

A waitress was on her way to the kitchen with a tray-balancing act of empty dishes. She stopped to watch what these jokers were up to.

Whitey got up and gave Mooko a man hug with a fist slap on the back.

"Salut, mon ami," Whitey said.

"You not sill doin' that Frenchy bullshit?"

Whitey smiled and held both palms up.

"Let's get some food, man. Kitchen closes at 10." Whitey said.

Mooko looked at his watch. "Eight hours and 37 minutes. 586 miles," he said.

Forty-five minutes after Mooko had plopped his formidable bulk into the booth and wiped a small mound of fried shrimp and clams off his plate, washed down with one pint of draft beer and another half still on the table, Mooko was grinning at Whitey and shaking his head.

"I got nothing personal 'gainst your old team here," Mooko said, jerking his head toward a window of the restaurant, "but might be a few Pittsburgh fans *dee-lighted* to see that place go crumbling away. Long as nobody gets hurt," he added, tilting his head forward and offering a serious gaze to his friend.

Whitey shook his head adamantly. He made a gesture of crossing his heart, then held up his right hand. "Any chance of that, it's 'no go.' The play gets scrubbed," he said.

"Accidents happen. You got to plan for mistakes," Mooko said. "Back to this 'pro' you been talkin about. How well you know this guy?"

"That's where I really need *your* help. He's started doing some prelim, checking the place out. Now he's telling me on the phone," Whitey said, pausing and glancing around to be sure that no one else was listening.

"Before I called you couple days ago, my guy tells me," Whitey lowered his voice, "the Mothership is *very* secure. Good electronics and cameras. The crew will need help. And more money."

Whitey continued, "Besides you coming with me to meet this guy, and he is *one weird cat*, ain't that some of what you do? Security, cameras and stuff?"

Now Mooko was shaking his head. "No, we have IT genius boys who handle all that. I'm just a good lookin, civic-minded muscle guy the boss likes to have around."

"But you can get a *read* on this AC guy. Told him I have a friend who's in 'security' who can help us. Even if you can't really do anything, which he ain't gonna know, you can hear what he's got to say, you might know somebody," Whitey said. "Plus, he gets a look at you, might slow him down coupla steps if he's trying some hide the ball hustle on me."

The two men stared at one another in silence.

Finally, lifting his beer glass from the table and taking a swallow, Mooko pinched the fingers of his left hand and moved them slowly back and forth across his chin. He shook his head, smiled again, then sat back.

"Okay. I'll go with you to meet the guy. Sounds to me, based on all you sayin so far, this project goes anywhere, we be lookin to recruit a couple more players," Mooko said.

Whitey nodded and picked up his own drained glass.

"Now, tell me about your connection to this AC. And where's the juice coming from to cover the game?"

"That your guy?" Mooko asked. It was the following morning after they'd met at the Red Wing. Whitey nodded.

"Eyes sensitive to artificial light? What's with the glasses?" Mooko said. It was 10 a.m. and the inside of the Wunder Mart was as bright as the first day of summer at Revere Beach.

Whitey shrugged. "I didn't ask," he said.

AC watched Whitey and some new guy walking in his direction. He waited. The meeting spot was a bench directly across from Men's Shoes. As the two came closer, AC stood, removed the mirror sunglasses, pulled his fatigue T-shirt above his stomach to wipe the lenses. He put the glasses back on. The man with Whitey reminded AC of an Army buddy in Afghanistan, a guy everyone called Smokey, as in "The Bear," because of his immense size.

"Gentlemen," AC said.

"Mister Vice President," Whitey said, "How's the quail hunting?"

AC gave him a thumbs up, then with both hands pretended to hold up an over-under 20-gauge, tracked across the ceiling of the store and jerked his shoulder as though he'd pulled off a shot.

"Mooko," Whitey gestured with a tilt of his head, then added, "AC."

No one shook hands.

"Let's go look at some paint," AC said, turning and walking in a direction away from the shoe department. Whitey and Mooko fell in behind him. For the next 10 minutes, AC Cahill walked and talked at the same time, a surprisingly soft-spoken, informal monologue explaining what would happen next, what he needed, where and when the subsequent steps would occur.

It was all precisely detailed and recited without notes.

Lifting different cans of paint from the shelves and replacing them while he talked, AC could have been giving a consumer lecture on the merits of latex versus acrylic. At one point he stopped and held up a six-pack of paint roller covers. He sniffed the plastic wrap, then turned the package over and pretended to be reading about the bright orange synthetic covers.

"If these were sticks of dynamite," he said, "we'd be using a whole crate of 'em. And I'm gonna need *two* helpers," he held up two fingers for emphasis, "who can move fast and not be stepping on their own dicks."

Whitey was aware that other shoppers had been giving Mooko the eye, but he played it cool. For his part, Mooko was nodding and smiling as though AC was explaining the benefits of domestic tranquility through proper home maintenance. AC placed the package of roller covers back on their hanger. He pushed the sunglasses up onto his forehead, swiveled left, then right, and pointed.

"There's a woman over there giving out samples of ice cream," he said. "Come on." Looking directly at Whitey, he added, "I'll give you the scoop on the added expenses. This is getting serious, gentlemen."

The unofficial consumers' stroll through the aisles of Wunder Mart marched on, AC Cahill, tour director.

20

MAYBE BABY

Shauntay was in top form. Whitey was considering a vitamin supplement, maybe one of those herbal extracts or a performance-enhancing pill.

Plans for the evening ahead included: Shauntay going to meet a new contact, a woman, referred to her by a longtime friend, Stefan. For Whitey, taking Jasmine out for an extended walk was at the top of the agenda. Then he'd thought about seeing a man about a plan, an encore visit.

"It's just like I told you the other evening, take your time. Get all the kinks worked out," Shauntay said. "Nobody with half a brain will buy into something that looks incomplete. But. . . ."

Whitey waited. She was applying lip gloss, leaning in close to the mirror.

"*But. . . ?*" Whitey said, holding out both arms, beckoning.

Shauntay dabbed her lips, placed the tiny brush back in the tube and dropped the tube into her purse. She turned to look at him.

"There's a woman. Stefan arranged a meeting. Says she has more money than God." Shauntay did not tell Whitey that she knew who the woman was and that she, too, believed that the woman had resources well above some of the lower-tier, affluent Bostonians.

"If you right about that, she ain't gonna put no money on the table to slow down ticket sales at the Fox Bowl!" Whitey said.

Shauntay restrained herself. Here she is trying to humor her man, maybe even get someone to throw some funds into the pot, and all he can do is second-guess her initiative. She decided to let him yap, but no more than another minute.

Yap, he did. "I been thinking on ways to do this," he said, recalling how excited Shauntay had become when he'd first mentioned the fantasy. They'd been in bed and the discussion had prompted overtime. When he'd said, "boom" in his deepest voice, then whispered "I'm gonna blow up the Fox Bowl," she had oohed, *twice*, and wouldn't let Whitey get out of the sack.

That was part of the reconciliation after the fight over his having shown too much attention to the young women on the sidewalk, which was perhaps the 87th time he'd done something that dumb. Now, he had another chance *not* to fuck up again and maybe Shauntay could get some money.

"And the best way to work it," he said, "is I need a small crew to help. I already found the guy who can do the job, a real pro. But he's not doin jack shit if I don't have the money and if I can't get a crew together."

Shauntay could tell by his tone and movements that, if she let him, Whitey was going to ramble through a step-by-step concept for the next hour. She didn't have the time. Walking across the bedroom to her desk, she flipped open a laptop computer, tapped a couple of keys and motioned for Whitey to come to the desk.

"What?" he said.

"Sit," she said, pulling the chair out. "Let me show you something."

Whitey sat down. Shauntay stretched her arms around his shoulders, sorta like a golf pro showing someone how to grip a club, and she tapped keys on the computer. Up on the screen, in all caps, came the words WHITEY'S BIG PLAN TO GO BOOM.

He stared at the screen. There was this little vertical line blinking at the end of the word BOOM. It had been awhile since he'd done anything on an actual computer, everything he needed could be handled on his phone.

Pressing her breasts against the back of his shoulders, Shauntay said, "It's easy. Just *type.*" She tapped keys then deleted what she'd typed: "What you gonna do. Don't stop. Put everything in there. All of it."

Whitey stared at the screen. The little vertical line was still blinking, now below the words Shauntay had typed.

"When I come home, I will read what you wrote and clean it up so that it makes sense. We can talk about it." She gave a light kiss to his right ear and pulled away from him.

Whitey slowly moved his hands closer to the keyboard but made no attempt to type anything.

"Don't forget Jasmine. And when you come back from her walk, keep typing. Don't need to turn it off. Whatever you write will be saved, automatically." She had her purse and her keys.

Whitey sat in front of the computer as though he was part of a sculpture exhibit at the Museum of Fine Arts—Man at Keyboard.

Before going out the door, Shauntay picked up Jasmine, gave her a nuzzle and some kiss, kiss sounds, returned to Whitey, where she gave him a quick, delicate grope in the groin and pointed at the laptop.

"Write your plan, baby." She was out the door and Jasmine was now at his feet, looking up.

Pecking slowly and studying the symbols and words on the different keys, Whitey struggled for nearly an hour. Some of what he typed made sense, but most of what he wrote didn't have the correct spacing and he kept getting stuck with all capital letters. It was only when he'd returned from pee-and-poop patrol with Jasmine that he figured out the best way to proceed was to type as though he were sending a text message. No worry about punctuation or spelling, these red lines kept showing up under a lot of the words he typed. Shauntay said that she would clean it up. Great.

On that 15-inch screen in front of him, a marginally coherent plan struggled to come together. By the time Whitey finished, what he'd written was almost clear enough to understand, at least he thought so. He ended his effort by tapping the $ key repeatedly and ended with exclamation points.

$$$$!!!

Late the following morning, Shauntay had a surprise for Whitey when he'd arrived back at the condo: a cleanly typed, edited and readable version of what he had hacked at the previous night.

It ran just over 300 words, properly spaced and with several bullet points. She didn't use the WHITEY'S BIG PLAN heading, instead she'd simply typed at the top of the page, Fox Bowl - The Plan. At the bottom of the page, she'd concluded not with exclamation points, but with one word and a question mark.

Budget?

After Whitey read *this* plan, he stood and gave Shauntay a hug.

"This is great," he said, kissing her forehead.

She took the sheet of paper from him, folded it like a letter that was going to be mailed, then slipped it into her purse.

"This is really for me," she said. "Something tells me that you and your 'expert' don't need no summary of what you're up to. But I need it. You know what I said about anyone with half a brain?"

Whitey looked at the folded sheet of paper sticking out of the top of Shauntay's purse, then he looked at her but said nothing.

"Different people invest in different ventures for their own reasons," she said. "Maybe one of those people with *too goddamn much money* will like this plan."

21

VALUED CUSTOMER

Whitey and Mooko were seated in the bar area of the Red Wing drinking Sam Adams Summer Ale and sharing a Fisherman's Platter entrée. The discussion had turned goofy as Whitey explained what he'd learned from AC Cahill's unusual habitation.

Mooko: "Whad'ya think might be the word back at corporate headquarters they get wind that a manager's enabling a long-term squatter behind the local Wunder Mart?" He shook his head and laughed, adding, "Really suck the wind right outa his chances for promotion, huh?"

Whitey: "You think? Or, maybe get him transferred to Bumfuk, Texas. I'm tellin ya, he says the guy—the store manager—owes him 'big time.' I didn't ask how. Second trip I went to see him, he's got a little propane stove and he's cooking friggin turkey burgers. Even has one of those gravity showers inside the place. And a boat porta potty."

Mooko: "Probably got a discount from the manager."

Whitey: "Who knows. Then he has these *two* big flat screen TVs mounted above the weight bench. Crazy."

Mooko: "Think he has WiFi?"

"Full moon and flying pigskins, campers. Now the Forecast." The theme music tonight was the Colonel Bogey march from the old movie *The Bridge on the River Kwai.*

The host, whistling along with the all-male chorus and Sousa-style march, eventually introduced himself as Sir Alec Guinness-Stout, the new Vice President of Scheduling of American Football in the UK.

"And leave those patriotic cans of *whatever-lite* it is you're drinking at home, men. We'll show you some real beer." The music came up, the canned 617-544-two-five, two-five announcement repeated in echo, followed by another, "Now . . . the Forecast."

Announcer: "It would also be my advice not to be telling real football hooligans that their beer is too warm. Order a pint and shut up.

First up tonight, Pittsburgh, PA. Okay. Give me an Iron City. You're on the radio."

Caller: "Hi. Thanks for taking my call."

Sir Alec: "It is our pleasure. What's on your mind?"

Caller: "Don't you think there should be more women reffing games?"

Sir Alec: "Ah, sure. Why not?"

Caller: "When I was a kid playing Pop Warner, my mom was at every game. She knew as much as any ref I ever saw."

Sir Alec: "I'll just bet she did. Tell me something. Ever recall your mother being asked to leave a game before it was over?"

The man on the line and the host went at it for another minute before the Pittsburgh caller got the hook.

"Think about it," Sir Alec intoned. "You have some 300-pound defensive lineman sitting on the bench grumbling that the ref is just like his mother."

Silence for five seconds, then another call.

"Portsmouth, New Hampshire. You're on the air."

Jack the Cabbie was queued-up with other drivers at the curb of Terminal E near the Arrivals gate at Logan International. Listening to the radio and the host doing a passable British theatrical accent, Jack was bringing up Alec Guinness films in his head.

"Jesus," he said to himself. "He must've made more than anybody of that era. Plus, all those years on stage." Jack had never seen any of the TV stuff Guinness did, but had heard about some great spy series from BBC. *Maybe get the DVDs when I go out West?*

The radio host had moved on to another caller.

"*Lawrence of Arabia*," Jack said aloud "*Doctor Zhivago. Cromwell. Kafka!*" There were a bunch of Star Wars movies, Obi-Wan something or other, that Jack had never seen. *What the hell was that about?*

Passengers rolling suitcases and carts were coming out of the terminal. Jack turned the volume down on the radio, started his engine and prepared to move forward.

Trooper Julie Egan had decided to hit the Red Wing for a late supper. She'd been there twice previously, but early in the day. Why not check out the locals?

Taking a seat at the bar, there were only half a dozen other customers. A man and a woman sat at a small table, an older guy and a young boy at the counter to her left, and two men at another table in the corner. Most of the patrons were over in the restaurant side. The two guys in the corner were laughing.

"Something to drink?" the man behind the bar asked. Julie knew his name was Dave.

"You have iced tea?" Julie said.

"Yep. With lemon?

"Sure. And could I see a menu, please?"

Specials were written on a white board above the bar, but Julie didn't want deep fried seafood or a heavy meal. Cabbie Jack had told her to try the Chicken Loaded Cheesy Tots, one of his favorites, with bacon, nacho cheese, sour cream and scallions.

Not tonight. She was more in the mood for lighter fare, a Caesar salad or antipasto, maybe.

"Topo Gigio back there thinks he's in Rome. Or Paris," the older guy seated next to her piped up. He nodded in the direction of the two men at the corner table.

"Excuse me. How's that?" Julie said.

"Every time he comes in, it's 'Bonjour, mon ami' or 'Au revoir.' He's about as French as that mustard," he said, again the head gesture, this time to condiments on the bar in front of Julie.

The old man had a tone suggesting that he was totally unimpressed with the well-dressed African American guy in the corner. Trooper Egan didn't ask for an assessment on the other man, who looked as though he was someone's bodyguard—maybe a football player.

"Do you know the story about five French kittens in a leaky boat?" said the young boy seated next to the old guy. Julie leaned forward so she could see the kid. He looked to be about seven or eight years old, maybe a grandson.

The old man turned to the boy. They'd been sharing a pizza.

"No, Lucas. I *don't* know that story."

"Un, deux, trois, quatre, cinq," the kid said, big eyes and big smile.

"That's very good," Julie said.

Dave brought the iced tea and took her order. She went for the salad. The old guy and the kid were finished and got up to leave, Gramps leaving a five-dollar bill for a tip.

After a few minutes, the two men at the corner table got up to leave. Sure enough, the character previously dubbed Topo Gigio gave a finger pistol shot to Dave behind the bar and said, "Au revoir."

Julie watched them. She felt her teeth crunching a garlicky crouton.

22

WE'LL SEE

Shauntay took a small sip of the Shanghai Fizz cocktail. "Yum," she said to her drinking partner, a woman perhaps five years older.

"This is . . . *really* good."

"It's the freshly squeezed lime juice and the champagne. I don't actually care about the gin," the woman replied. She held up her fluted glass for a toast. "To fashion. And beautiful women." The glasses clinked; both women drank.

Shauntay placed her glass on the table and dabbed at her mouth with a lime green paper napkin. She studied her partner, someone she certainly knew about but had never met in person until 10 minutes ago. Though the woman might be a few years older, possibly 40, she was absolutely gorgeous.

"Here's a question. Why are some women considered beautiful, and other women are referred to as 'stunning'?" Shauntay asked.

"Some are both. I think it depends on who is making the assessment," the woman said.

Shauntay laughed. "How about if it comes from someone anonymous?"

The woman shrugged and held her hands up. "My mother instilled in my sisters and me, 'always consider the source'."

"A few nights ago, I was leaving the shooting range. . . ."

"You go to a *shooting range*?" the woman interrupted, nearly spilling her drink as she placed the glass back on the table.

Shauntay nodded. "Every Friday evening. Sometimes on the weekend, too."

"That is remarkable," the woman said.

"Anyway, I'd just finished and was getting ready to leave when the manager motioned for me to wait. He came over and handed me a note that someone had left for me." Shauntay shook her head and took another sip of the Shanghai Fizz. The woman waited.

"It was folded over and stapled closed." Shauntay's smile went full wattage. "I didn't open it until I got outside."

"What did the note say?"

"Well, whoever *wrote* it must've thought he was sending a text message. It read, 'U R the most stunning wmn I hve ever seen.'" Shauntay laughed again, then added, "He R making me . . . *L-O-L*."

"Not the most romantic overture, I guess," the woman said. "Any idea who sent it to you?"

Shauntay's eyebrows went up and she held her hands out. "Could be the manager for all I know."

"What did you do with the note? You should ask him."

"I threw it in a trash container in the parking lot," Shauntay said. "As you say, *not* very romantic."

"*But* . . . an admirer. Better keep your eyes open when you go back to the range."

The woman who ordered the champagne cocktails and offering the toast also knew about Shauntay. From a distance, she not only appreciated Shauntay's beauty and, for the present, her mid-level modeling career, but she perceived a certain touch of class. And she certainly believed that Shauntay had a promising future. Not as one of the runway anorexics, who landed a good agent or manager, but as someone who, beauty aside, would find her niche in the world.

But they were not here to talk modeling. Stefan, who had carefully orchestrated this meeting, had convinced both women that they should meet. More-or-less a confidante for each of them, he stressed the need for a face-to-face conversation. And here they were.

Chitchat aside, Shauntay was not only struck by the woman's being more attractive in person than any photo conveyed, but also how contemplative and reserved she seemed to be. Not an airhead.

"We should look at the menu," the woman said. "Then I want to hear all about your man. And this special project. Stefan says that I might find it, shall we say, intriguing.

Shauntay rolled her eyes and reached for her glass. "My man. Oh, my, my. Where do I start?" She took another sip of the Shanghai Fizz.

Nearly two hours later, dinner over and the last of a bottle of Delle Venezie Reserve Pinot Grigio from Italy on the table between them, with most other diners having left, Shauntay was finally talked out.

The two women were now quiet, perhaps the real sizing up coming down to these final moments. Whether either woman would thank their mutual friend or lambaste him for exercising poor judgment in arranging this meeting, that remained unknown.

Shuantay took a sip of her wine and shifted in her chair. The waiter had left the check half an hour ago and she now reached for it. The woman gently pushed her hand away and took the leather check presentation folder for herself.

"This is my treat," the woman said, placing a black credit card inside the folder.

"Thank you," Shauntay said.

After the waiter had taken the check and her credit card, the woman poured the remaining wine from the bottle into their glasses. She proposed a toast to Shauntay.

"It all sounds . . . *just a little crazy*," she said, with a laugh, "but count me in." She extended her glass and added, "Here's to a successful . . . boom."

They clinked, drank, smiled at one another, Shauntay shaking her head and offering, "We'll see."

The waiter returned with the credit card print out and left it on the table. As she signed her name, the woman looked up at Shauntay, holding the pen above the slip.

"You should know, money is not an issue here. When everything is ready, tell me what you need. You will have cash within 24 hours."

Forty minutes southwest of Boston, leaving the Red Wing after her own late-evening dinner, Julie spotted the men from the corner table in the bar now out in the parking lot, talking. They'd left the diner some 20 minutes before she did.

Pulling the state police cruiser around to head home, her headlights swept over the two men and the yellow Corvette.

The big guy was pacing slowly back and forth, arms folded, while the other man rested against the back of the car, arms moving. He appeared to be doing all the talking.

Back at her lavish Newbury Street digs, Shauntay carried Jasmine to the elevator for a final walk of the night. When they reached the lobby, she clipped the leash to the dog's faux-diamond-studded collar and off they went.

Reflecting on the getting-to-know-you minuet she'd had throughout the evening, Shauntay thought that she knew the real motivation behind the woman's interest in becoming involved. She was also pretty sure that Stefan, from the beginning, had guessed it as well.

Jasmine squatted at the edge of a strip of grass near the entrance to Shimmy & Silk. The dog was not looking at her when Shauntay whispered to herself, "Yes, indeed, *we will see*."

23

AWESOME

If there were security video archives in the Fox Bowl complex, it might take multiple viewings to pick out AC Cahill. Even with a clear, 10 o'clock in the morning surveillance with few other people around.

Nattily dressed in an ivory, off-the-rack summer-weight suit—on sale this week at Wunder Mart for $179 (before manager's discount)—with a powder-blue shirt and clip-on striped necktie, AC also wore a pair of what used to be called black patent-leather slip-ons. *And*, he crowned himself with a dark-brown hairpiece, likely from the Marv Albert Collection.

Turning the key to off, he placed his mirror sunglasses on the passenger seat of his 1997 Honda Civic hatchback. AC looked at himself in the rearview mirror. He was not in a convivial mood. He was, in fact, pissed.

Despite his ultra-polite overtures and his carefully crafted counterfeit press credentials, he had been told by a team media spokesperson that they no longer offered public tours of the Fox Bowl. Contrary to nostalgic videos still floating around on the internet from the 1990s, he would be unable to join in a high-fives $79.95 Super Pirates Personal Fan Tour.

Fuck 'em, he thought. He'd just have to organize a self-guided walk around. Audio guide not required.

AC started with a quick pass through the gift, souvenir and team accessories shop; checked out the trophies, game footballs, photos, old equipment and more memorabilia than one might imagine.

Pausing for long minutes and looking through the upper level windows at the colossal sports edifice outside, AC snapped photos with his phone. He eventually found his way to a small theater showing a film on the history of the Pirates and the stadium.

There were only two other people in the theater when he entered, an older man and probably his wife. AC took a front row seat, dead center, less than 10 yards from the big screen.

AC sat mesmerized. The film lasted just over 15 minutes. By the time it ended, tears were rolling down his cheeks. And AC wasn't a serious football fan. He followed the Bruins. Although he had known about Whitey's signing bonus back in the day courtesy of an Army pal, also from Louisiana.

Sitting in a booth of the main dining room at the Red Wing at lunch time, Whitey didn't recognize the man coming toward him.

"Can't do it," the man said, taking a seat, which made Whitey realize that it was AC. It was the voice. Shaking his head, like a bobblehead that moved only laterally, not speaking, AC held up both hands. Now he looked like a bobblehead dressed in a suit inside a goal post.

Whitey said nothing.

A waitress appeared at the booth. She was looking at the wig. AC looked at her. "You have chocolate milk?" he asked.

"Yes."

"Big glass. No straw."

Turning back to Whitey, AC shrugged his shoulders and now held one hand up. "They've got this movie, dude. About the team's history. Clips with different fans talking about it all. I used to visit my grandfather down the Cape. He was a cranberry farmer. One of those fans in that movie, coulda been *Gramps*." AC left out the part about his tears.

Whitey remained silent.

"And the place is about three times larger than I thought. I never been there before, It's awesome. Like Disney World North, man!" AC said.

"What you want to do, even *my version* of the plan, simply will not work."

"Too bad," Whitey said, as he placed five mustard-colored straps of $100 bills on the table. AC looked down at the cash. Fifty-grand, just like he'd told the man. The waitress returned with the glass of chocolate milk.

Whitey covered the money with a napkin before she arrived at the booth.

Whitey and AC spent an hour at the Red Wing, vacuuming cheeseburgers, onion rings, two glasses of chocolate milk for AC, and one draft beer for Whitey.

Following AC's enthusiastic review of the video at the Fox Bowl, Whitey went through his own commentary and reiterated that his objective was to do "serious damage" to the stadium to "send a message," and that he expected AC to devise the best plan that would accomplish that and cause no physical harm. "To anyone," he added.

"And the *message* would be what, dude?" AC replied. Chocolate milk on his upper lip, ketchup on the fingers of his left hand, he resembled Alfred E. Neuman sans diastema. It might have been the hairpiece.

Whitey glared icily through AC. Right through him. "Fuck you, Pirates! *That's* the motherfuckin message."

Whitey once again removed the straps of cash from a small black leather dopp kit that he kept handy on the seat next to him. Gripping the five bundles in his right hand, he reached under the table and placed the money on the bench next to AC.

"We gonna do this or what?" Whitey whispered.

AC looked down at the cash, then back to Whitey. Swigging the final drop of milk, wiping his mouth with a napkin and eating the last onion ring, he stuffed the cash into the pockets of his new suit coat and rose from the table.

"We'll talk, dude. Gimme coupla days," AC said. He turned and left the diner.

Whitey sipped the last of his beer. He thought about ordering a BBQ pizza to go, then decided against it. He would stop by Dunkin on the way back to his condo and get a cheesecake doughnut. And get another look at Brandi's bouncy young rear end.

Parking his car at the far end of the Wunder Mart lot, behind the Garden Center near the rent-a-trucks, AC removed the hairpiece, took off the necktie and jacket, and walked to his customized steel container home.

Stripped down to shorts, a T-shirt and flip flops, he began one of his thrice daily weightlifting routines. Normally, he wore earbuds and listened to music or had some action video going on one of the flat screens. But he needed to concentrate.

By the time he'd finish 30 minutes of warm up, squats, bench presses, bent leg crunches and finished with more stretching, AC had worked out in his head what, realistically, could be done at the Fox Bowl.

He created a mental checklist of what would be needed and the kind of support team that would be required. Next step, a phone call to The Mayor, who would help source the explosives and maybe recruit some interference guys.

But the real test of the seriousness for the commitment level from one Antoine LeBlanc and friends would be the "full package" price—one million, all inclusive.

If I'm gonna fuckin do this, it's a one and done and I'm gone, thank you.

The Mayor wasn't surprised to get the call. He'd expected it earlier. AC explained on the phone about his near meltdown following the viewing of a promotional film at the Fox Bowl Visitors Center. He'd said the film damn near brought him to tears, revealing how as a kid he used to visit Grampy who lived on a cranberry bog down the Cape, with the old man and practically everyone else then thinking of the new professional football team as the best thing since the *Mayflower* dropped anchor.

"He gave me 50 thou," AC said. "This all comes together, my original bid is right on target. We're still lookin at a million."

"I told him it was gonna be big bucks," O'Connolly said.

"As did I. Now we'll see if he has the juice."

O'Connolly: "Whad'ya need from me?'

AC: "I need a contact for help getting material. And maybe a little distraction while I get the explosives in place. Probably need two or three guys. I have an idea. No real danger, just some goofballs. Only need em for an hour or two, late at night."

O'Connolly: "Not a problem."

AC: "Let me think on it some more."

Barring a surprise visit from a reporter with *The Boston Globe* Spotlight Team, Michael O'Connolly was not anticipating issues that couldn't be dealt with. He could make another hand-off with a Providence connection for AC Cahill.

Reflecting on AC's situation and using a scale of zero to 10, The Mayor decided that the amenities of his own motel room, as compared, say, to a seaworthy shipping container, were climbing by the hour. Maybe an eight.

24

TAXI SQUAD

Whitey was parked next to two dumpsters at the far end of the lot at the Red Wing. Resting his butt on the Corvette, he nervously tossed the nerf ball back and forth, one hand to the other, occasionally spiraling it up high and then stretching to catch it.

The diner would be closing in a few minutes. The plan called for Mooko to arrive before 10 o'clock. He was bringing two men with him all the way from Pittsburgh. Whitey didn't know the guys but was assured by Mooko that they were "walk ons" with a lot of experience.

As soon as they arrived, Whitey would get into Mooko's car for a drive-by just up the road—Route 1 and the Fox Bowl. Hard to know about traffic they might encounter off the highway. Adjacent to the stadium, in a perimeter much like a concrete rampart, there were a variety of business establishments, including a cinema complex. Some would be closed others would still have customers this time of the evening.

The parking lots ran in a semi-circular pattern around the front end and to the sides of the place. Much of it was fenced off, accessible only on game days or when some other event was taking place. Whitey knew the area well. His most recent visit had been also at night just a week earlier with the eccentric "AC" Cahill, before AC conducted his self-tour.

Once Whitey had assuaged AC's misgivings, he believed now that The Project was approaching a crucial countdown period. In two weeks, three maximum it would be all systems go—or shit the bed and let's go home. Game over.

The remaining hurdle was what AC had referred to as additional "AA" costs, as in "artistic alteration." Another 250 grand, which would put the cost just over the original one-million-dollar cap they had agreed on.

Pulling in the earlier cash installments had not been as difficult as Whitey had feared, thanks to Shauntay and a mystery benefactor. Another quarter-mil might cause a shutdown.

Whitey had decided that before he would spring this latest news on Shauntay, he and Mooko and the walk-ons, would make a reconnaissance run, then go see AC over at the Wunder Mart. Once everybody liked everybody else, or at least agreed that they could function as a squad, he could then worry about getting the additional cash.

Whitey looked at his watch: 9:58. He threw the nerf ball onto the passenger seat when a dark green Toyota Tacoma pick up with a tonneau cover and Pennsylvania plates pulled up behind his Corvette.

Mooko was riding shotgun in the truck and lowered his window. The guy driving had on a black and gold knit hat. There was another man in the back seat. Whitey couldn't see him clearly.

Mooko got out, stretched, rolled his neck, gave Whitey a fist bump, then opened the rear passenger door.

"Hop up front," Mooko said. "You're the navigator. I'll get in back."

As soon as Whitey had his seat belt fastened and Mooko had closed the door, the driver began slowly turning the vehicle around.

"Say hello to Spike and Goose," Mooko said. "Boys, this is Antoine 'The Bayou Flash' LeBlanc. Known to all his close friends as Whitey."

Spike and Goose? Can't be their real names. Whitey sized up the two men as much as he could in the darkened interior of the cab. *Maybe they had played football somewhere.*

"Thanks for making the trip," Whitey said.

Not that anyone outside their immediate families gave a shit, their real names were, Aaron "Spike" Gallegos and Karol "Moose" Erjavek, local buds from the Monongahela Valley region of southwestern Pennsylvania and West Virginia. Rough country. Tough buckaroos.

The four pranksters headed south on Route 1.

The Mayor called on one of his *other* connections in Providence. Rocco had provided a contact for acquiring the explosives. O'Connolly didn't want to bother him with AC's trivial request for some goofballs for a late-night run.

"Find me two or three young guys with pickup trucks," AC had said in their most recent phone chat. O'Connolly had come through.

He knew a guy who knew a guy. The second guy was a retired vocational ed instructor who had a deep roster of young men who were "into automotive arts" as he liked to say. Some of these young men were legit and had gone on to successful entrepreneurship, or at least steady employment. A few, however, had been wandering off in other directions, occasionally handling after-hours extraction and redistribution.

It was through the latter group that The Mayor was able to compile a list of players with the right attitude. They could be available on short notice for an evening of rollicking fun and quick cash.

The Mayor would wait for further instructions from Wunder Mart command central.

Should the Walpole police happen to be patrolling the Mart late on this Friday night, they might be puzzled to spot a group of men gathered out beyond the 24-foot-high LED lights illuminating the sweeping blacktop parking lot.

Five men, to be exact: Antoine LeBlanc, Mooko and his two roadies, Spike and Moose, all listening to a running commentary from one AC Cahill, who was pacing in front of them like a drill instructor.

AC had been ticking off steps of a plan that he would execute for a late-night visit to the Fox Bowl. The exact date yet to be determined, but it would happen soon. The crew listening to him right now would be crucial to any chance of pulling off the mission.

"I'll take care of getting everything needed for the job. Once we know the date," AC said, looking at Whitey, "we get back together the night before and do a little run-through. A scenario proofing, so to speak."

Moose glanced at Spike. *What the fuck is scenario proofing?* Spike couldn't actually read his mind, but he'd been around

Moose long enough to absorb the gist of his thoughts, so he offered a barely perceptible shake of the head.

AC had also picked up on Moose's look. "Save your questions. We'll cover it all the night before the dance."

With that, AC smiled, saluted the four men, and began walking backwards. Before turning around to head off to his cozy domicile, he stopped abruptly and pointed a finger back at the group: "Antoine. Keep your phone totally on, dude. We'll talk soon."

Whitey nodded. They all watched AC pull the mirror sunglasses off his forehead and adjust them on the bridge of his nose before strolling out under the bright lights and heading across the parking lot.

25

BIFF NO. 9

Much to the annoyance of some other hackies and perhaps a few Uber drivers, Jack the Cabbie had decided to spend the summer in Boston. He was a popular guy and knew how and where to get the best fares. Regular customers knew to look for a driver wearing a loud Hawaiian shirt and playing a ukulele in the taxi rank.

On this particularly warm evening, however, hauling people to Logan Airport, or taking long runs all the way to Mohegan Sun, was not what he had in mind. If word got out that he was hanging out with a young, attractive state trooper of the female variety, Jack might be taking long runs to Philadelphia. Or Baltimore.

But that's what he was doing—hanging out with Trooper Julie Egan. Off the meter.

After a long and casual dinner with perhaps too much to drink, at least for her, Julie tried to maintain the approach that she had adopted after the first morning when she met Jack: "listen more, talk less." The man clearly had a lot of worldly experience and was not shy about sharing it with her.

Although she'd spent much of the previous evening wondering why yesterday there had appeared to be more activity than normal for a lazy Wednesday afternoon at Fox Bowl. More trucks arriving, more humans scurrying around, just busier. But she was still relatively new on the beat—with a limited backlog of personal on-site observation. So, she had waited as long as she could before bringing it up with Jack.

"Speaking of comings and goings," said Trooper Egan, now back up in the camo blind and sipping morning espresso. She pointed at a convoy of tractor trailers rumbling by, many loaded with Honey Bucket portable restrooms.

"What's up?" she added.

"Game Day," Jack said. "Mr. Fox, the owner, his way of thanking the adoring fans. Middle of July, lets the poor bastards uncork some of that bottled-up Pirates fanaticism between the Super Brawl and the actual opening kickoff of the new season."

"How many people will be here?" Julie asked

"Oh, it depends," Jack said. "Hundred thousand anyway—that's on an off year. When the team wins the Big Game, as they did this year, upwards of a quarter-million could show up. Veritable throngs of rabid aficionados!"

The Cabbie asked Trooper Egan if she would like to take a tour: "Give you an excuse to poke around incognito—always my favorite mode of exploration."

She said, "So I gather."

"Let me make a phone call."

"Melinda? My niece Julie is visiting from out of town. Yeah, the smart college girl. Vassar. Big Pirates fan—*big.*" Just making stuff up as his mouth moved. Complete fabrication. Spewing lies. "Acting presidential" he called it.

"Say, may I impose on you to arrange for a tour on Game Day this Saturday? Hmm. Ah-ha. Okay. That should work. She'll be *thrilled.* I really appreciate it. I owe you one, Melinda. Come by for an espresso sometime. And be sure to wear that short leather cowgirl skirt. Makes you look ravishing!"

Jack put down his phone.

"I think you're all set. Media Relations ordered a dozen personal Game Day guides, but Melinda thinks the agency can send only eight or nine. Let's hope it's nine because she's tentatively assigned you Biff No. 9."

"Who?"

"Oh, come on—Biff Bradley! The Biffer. Star *quarterback?* Best ever and all that happy horseshit. None other than Golden Boy."

"What do you mean *the agency* is sending him?"

"Some outfit down the Cape. Stud Noir, I think it's called. Provincetown."

Jack explained that the celebrity modeling agency had a retainer from the Pirates to have a certain number of Biff Bradley lookalike models on standby year-round for various special functions and private tours of the stadium. Morning talk-show hosts, reptile politicians, hedge-fund cannibals, typically with their overdressed mistresses in tow wrapped in gold lamé jumpsuits.

"Everyone in the entourage gets a swag bag of Pirates-logo ceremonial trinkets and an 8x10 glossy photo of the fake Biff, complete with a fake signature. And they love it," he added.

Jack said the team even supplies the modeling agency with a voice coach and video of the real Biff so these actors can get his "talk and walk and all the mannerisms down."

"Do they know he's fake?"

"Some do, some don't. But either way it's a stroke of genius. Who *isn't* going into work Monday and crow about anyone less than the real Biff Bradley showing him around the Bowl?"

"I presume these guys are . . . gay."

"And ya would presume cor-r-r-ectly, mah dea*rrrr* lassie," Jack the Cabbie intoned in a dead-on Scottish accent.

Simple, Jack explained. Word gets out the real Biff Bradley is strolling through Game Day unchaperoned and the women would descend on him like Nip Zeros at Pearl Harbor. Team can't take that chance.

"Every supermarket tabloid in America would have some salacious story about a bored doctor's wife from Newton with fake boobs, getting all frisky and offering up a little oral pleasure out behind the goal posts in section 120," Jack imagined, shaking his head. "No way Media Relations wants to deal with that nightmare."

"Real or fake, I imagine," Julie quipped, beginning her descent to the parking lot and her cruiser.

Jack smiled and watched her prepare to depart.

"Brace your lovely self for an exuberant extravaganza," Jack yelled down as she started the engine in her patrol car. "Oh, on Saturday? Ditch the uniform."

Trooper Egan smiled back and gave Cabbie Jack a little two-finger salute before driving away and avoiding more of the incoming traffic.

26

GAME DAY

"**This is the Fox Den,** the Fox family suite when the team is in town," said tour guide Biff No. 9. "See this glass?" Biff tapped on the window. "Twelve and a half inches thick. A bomb could go off right below us and we'd be safe."

Biff No. 9 explained that the Foxes are dearly beloved around here because they saved football. The Pirates needed a new stadium, but they had trouble finding investors. "They were long-time losers, from the very first day they pissed off half of nascent Rex Sox Nation when they tore up the outfield one long-ago December at Fenway Park."

"The Pirates played at *Fenway*?" Julie, in civilian clothes, asked.

"Oh, yes, sure did, back in the '60s, for a year or two," her guide said. "Team was worthless. Joke of the League. Cellar dwellers."

Biff No. 9 expounded further on the Pirates' shaky history. When the team finally did get its own stadium, he recalled, a fan once sued them because a popcorn machine blew up in the stands. Another time the toilets stopped working. "Some bright guy who substituted a slide rule for a brain suggested that the solution was to flush all the toilets in the place, simultaneously."

"No—did that work?" Julie said.

"Ha! What do you think? They called it the Big Flush. I think there's a rapper calls himself that—might have even played here at the Bowl, right out on the field before us."

The Pirates, he continued, were all set to relocate to Florida, in cahoots with some Indian casino and a couple of shadowy financiers from Key Biscayne. The owners thought the casino angle would be a pretty good marketing gimmick. Plus use every high school in the state as a free farm system.

"The whole thing went south—pardon the pun—when some bodies were found in canal culverts along the Tamiami Trail. FBI moved in and rounded up the ringleaders. So that was that," Biff No. 9 said. "And that's when Mr. Fox stepped in. He had been approached earlier about joining a new investment group but declined. Didn't like the smell of the Florida deal. Told them his cash was tied up in family trusts, which most of it probably was. What he did have was land—the land you're looking at."

Turns out that Edward Wellington Fox, IV had leased 700 acres to the New England Pirates for 25 years—on the condition that they stay in Foxborough for 25 years. Over time, one by one, the original investors dropped out, bored with the project as the team continued its losing ways. But Mr. Fox hung in there. He quietly picked up their shares at bargain prices. Gradually, the team's fortunes turned around. And when the good times started rolling, he was in the driver's seat. "That's when we started calling him Mr. Big."

"Where did the land come from, I mean, originally?" Egan asked.

"English stole it from the Indians—the usual real estate transaction back in the 1600s," her tour guide said. "But more interesting is how the Fox got into Foxborough."

The still-quaint town was settled in 1704 but not incorporated until 1778, with the colonies still in treasonous revolt against the armies and navies of King George III, and their political future by no means certain. The locals, added Biff No. 9, were so appreciative of the staunch support of their colonial cause by one Charles James Fox—the Honourable Mr. Fox, Member of Parliament, Eton and Oxford man—that they named their little corner of the Commonwealth after him. All the way across the Atlantic.

Biff No. 9, breaking into an 18th century grandiloquent oration: "There is no man who hates the power of the Crown more, or who has a worse opinion of the Person to whom it belongs than I."

"You're standing inside a miracle of modern construction," the tour guide now explained, "with an unobstructed view of the playing field from literally every single seat in the house. Never been done before." He began reeling off a dizzying blizzard of statistics:

- Two million square feet of pure football fan joy. . . .
- More than 6,000 pieces of blue steel weighing 16,000 tons form the structure of the Fox Bowl. . . .
- Nearly 18,000 cubic yards of concrete poured. . . .
- Sixteen stories with 1,500 television monitors. . . .
- Two massive video boards—the south one alone 42 by 164 feet. . . .
- Five thousand dedicated employees run the place on any game day. . . .
- On-site kitchens serve more than a ton of Italian sausage and 186 gallons of clam chowder. . . ."

Julie's guide seemed to take such personal pride in the gargantuan football cathedral here in the land of provincial *baseball* worship, she thought, that one might believe that he had been the chief architect.

Then she was momentarily startled by the sound of a series of loud, rumbling explosions outside.

"That's the start of the battle of the pirate ships out on the flooded practice field," Biff the guide said, grinning. "Probably *Queen Anne's Revenge* setting off the first cannon charges. That was Blackbeard's ship, you know—near exact replica. Let's go down and take a stroll."

Biff No. 9 pushed the button for the ground floor. Halfway down the elevator came to a quiet halt. The door opened and two drunk-as-skunks insurance adjusters from Hartford holding drained bottles of Captain Morgan Spiced Rum tried to steady themselves, squinting through bloodshot eyes. One of them was wearing clip-on sunglasses with the left lens missing.

"Hey," the guy with the crooked glasses said with a slurred, sulfurous burp. "Aren't you . . . ?"

The elevator door closed smoothly in their red faces, leaving the pair of disheveled potbellied partiers behind.

"What the hell was *that?*" Julie asked.

"Oh, that was the Forbidden Floor. Notice how there was no marked level number?"

The elevator opened again, to a flood of sunshine. Out of nowhere a quartet of 250-pound tattooed bearded gym rats dressed like Vikings closed ranks and started parting the Red Sea of swooning and swarming fans. They were brandishing coiled bullwhips and rolling pins.

"Back off, heathens!" yelled one through a megaphone. "Don't make us badasses misbehave."

"No selfies!" bellowed another. "Mr. Bradley's in training."

Biff No. 9 turned around and whispered: "They're called the 'Worcester Bikers.' Mr. Big likes to have them around to scare the piss out of hipsters in skinny jeans." He put his forefinger to his lips and winked at Julie.

He's not kidding, she thought, taking in the sheer scope of the raucous and riotous party. *This is like Burning Man for action-starved football fans.*

The dueling pirate ships were booming in the background, sending great towers of white cannon smoke skyward. There were huge crackling bonfires, roasting pigs and turkeys on spits, tanker trucks spouting free beer, donkeys painted in Pirates colors, screeching peacocks chasing frenzied feral children, and a skeet range where you could blast away with 18th century blunderbusses at miniature footballs launched by mechanical cutouts of famous quarterbacks.

She heard shooters hollering out names in staccato, like some military roll call: Unitas! *Bam.* Starr! *Bam.* Montana! *Bam.* Bradshaw! *Bam.* Marino! *Bam.* Elway! *Bam.* . . .

Or, you could dig for pieces of eight in the official Buried Treasure Pit, up to your ankles in certified grade-A liquid cow shit trucked in from Vermont.

"Aye, matey—*keel-haul* the bastards!" cried a deep-throated peg-legged eye-patched ringmaster in a tricorne hat, standing above the crowd, gleaming saber drawn, in a game called Walk the Plank. All the onlookers watched a steady stream of participants—wobbly fans in handcuffs, rounded up by the booze patrol of men who wore red bandanas and Keith Richards' masks.

Balloons were rising and confetti falling. Word spread that Melania was flying in on Air Force One for the nightly fireworks.

Amidst the whirl and whorl, Julie Egan caught the wafting aroma, sizzle and smoke from a busy food stand: *My Other Cousin Manny's—New Bedford, Mass.*

"Linguica with grilled peppers and onions," Biff said. "Delicious. This joint is in Provincetown, too. Real Portuguese rolls. Right off the grill they'll burn your frickin tongue off. But they're so tasty you can't help yourself."

Julie said, *"Yummm,"* motioning to Biff to step right up.

"I can't be seen eating this stuff in public," he said through his helmet. "Gotta stick with decaf seaweed tea and free-trade fermented banana leaves. You know, keep up the image."

"That sucks," she said, handing 10 bucks to the heavyset woman in a white apron behind the counter.

"Price of fame," he said.

Julie made her way through the throngs following her guide. She stopped mid-bite.

Chase the Wench! read a hand-lettered sign hanging above a lineup of comely young women in period pirate costumes, all sitting relaxed in folding camp chairs with beverage holders in the armrests. Legs crossed and fluffy petticoats visible, all of the women seemed to be relaxed. Several were enveloped in vaping smoke.

Julie looked up at a larger-than-normal crow's nest draped in what looked like a small multicolored hot-air balloon.

"What's up there?" she asked one of the Worcester Bikers, a man named Norm who had long blonde hair and a large diamond ear stud. Biff No. 9 was momentarily distracted signing autographs.

"A waterbed, complete with a jellybean jar of candy-colored condoms," he replied, taking a quick swig from the engraved pewter flask in his hip pocket.

"For $500, guys over 50 get to choose their wench off the bench, then chase her up the rope ladder. All credit cards gladly accepted. Merican 'spress included."

"Why over 50?"

"And preferably overweight—so they'll never catch her."

"Do they ever?"

"Never seen it myself, ma'am, personally. I mean, them girls are trained gymnasts."

And if perchance a miracle happens, Norm the Biker told Julie the off-duty cop, and the guy manages to huff and puff his way to the top, there's a trap door to drop the moron down the waterslide and into the Crocodile Moat: "Fake crocs, a course. *Jaws*-style," he said.

"But most of these fools are so exhausted," Norm added, "they just collapse. They tumble into the netting strung below. Either way, happy customer ends up with a pair of perfumed panties stuffed into his mouth: Nice souvenir to pass around to his pals back home in the man cave."

"Oh, please," Julie said, rolling her eyes.

"Don't shoot the messenger, little lady," he said, throwing his hands in the air in who-*me?* fashion. "Guys will be jackasses. Remember that cover of *New York* magazine?

Julie looked puzzled.

"Dozen years ago, or so, Governor of New York, name a Spritzer or Swisher—a real shitkicker—patronized a supposed elite ring of prostitutes called the Emperor's Club. Five grand a pop. Turned out they was garden-variety hookers. Ha! Stupid sumbitch ended up on the cover of the magazine, standing there with a silly grin and an arrow pointing to his dick with the word BRAIN."

"This wench thing is just nuts," Julie said. "What if someone gets hurt?"

"Mr. Fox, as usual," answered the Biker, "has it covered. His personal helicopter is on full standby. Certified medevac team. Even got a volunteer priest aboard to perform last rites."

"Couple years back," Norm the Biker went on, "some loser *did* make it up the crow's nest—barely. The wench was holding on to him for dear life on the ladder, thinking he was having a heart attack. Had to airlift the sumbitch to the hospital in one of them slings wildlife biologists use to relocate those goddamn wild goats in the mountains out West. No shit."

"Did he die?"

"No, no, no. Simple case of dehydration. Choked on a Buffalo wing. Likely swallowed too much beer. Nurses gave him an IV. He was back at work Monday morning. Wife never got wind of his little adventure."

"How thoughtful," Julie said.

"Shows you the kind of class act Mr. Big is," the Worcester Biker said, wiping away a tear on the back of his hairy arm just above the dog-collar bracelet. "Ain't nothin too good for that man's fans. Nothin."

27

HOT AUGUST NIGHT

The music was the theme from *Rocky*. The horns came up for 10 seconds before the announcer offered, "Yo, sports fans. It is our official end-of- summer show." The phrase echoed and repeated multiple times, the music stayed under: "End-of-summer show . . . end-of-summer show."

"Your host for this special installment is . . . *Number. . . 20!*" Music up for three seconds, reverb on number 20.

"Loosen the laces on your spikes and settle back. We have all the calls you *missed* over the past three months." Music up for another 20 seconds and a chorus joined in, "*Trying hard now. . . .*"

Announcer: "We have maybe . . . a dozen or so of the best calls from the show going back to June. Even if you heard 'em, you'll wanna listen again. Tell your neighbors. . . ."

"Pack up the babies, and grab the old ladies and everyone goes. . . ." a clip from Neil Diamond's *Brother Love's Travelling Salvation Show* came up, then a quick segue back to Rocky's *Gonna Fly Now.*

Announcer: "Who am I?" The theme music faded, followed by the crowd cheering sound effect.

"There's been at least *one* of us in every sport you can think of," the announcer said. "But tonight, I am . . . Number 20. Just shy of four thousand-yards rushing, 25 touchdowns . . . and some impressive jewelry." Three seconds of silence, then he was back.

"Think about it, friends. We'll give it up at the end of the program. In the meantime, for your listening pleasure. . . . Now the Forecast. End-of-summer show." Pre-recorded excerpts of previous phone calls began to fill the airwaves.

"From Saugus. You're on the radio."

"Yeah, thanks for taking my call. You know, I listen to a bunch of shows all the time. In my car, out in the garage. Family trips, I got sports talk on the radio. My wife wears little foam earplugs and buries her nose in a book."

Announcer: "Smart woman."

Caller: "Yeah. She likes baseball. But you don't talk about. . . ."

Announcer: "You got it, pal. We do *not* talk about . . . America's Last Time."

Caller: "Yeah, anyway. I hear some of these other sports jocks. . . ."

Announcer: "Was that a pun?"

Caller: "Nah. DJs play music, right? You do a show about *sports*, makes you a sports jockey, correct?"

"Only if it supports what you're doing at the moment, would be my answer. *And* . . . you get a paid for it."

Caller: "Okay. So, seems to me, more and more of these shows, doesn't take long, somebody's calling in about politics and stuff. Pretty soon the sports jock is off to the nosebleed seats. He's giving the whole nine yards on why so-and-so shouldn't be running for office. Two minutes later, there's *another* caller picking up on what the jock was whining about."

Announcer: "It is a sad state of affairs, indeed. Probably doin' the same rant on his blog, huh?"

Caller: "I don't read blogs."

"Good for you. Now, can I offer a suggestion about the wife? For the next road trip?

"Sure. What's that?"

Announcer: "Pull a little fake with her. Switch to one of those religious stations. Then after a few miles, stop at the next rest area. Tell her you're going to get out and pray . . . for more shows like this one."

Click. Saugus caller gone.

Before the show limped to its final minutes, as promised, 10 more listeners had made it through. Some clips had been edited from the original broadcasts. Number 20 was going to squeeze in one more listener.

"*Now the Forecast.* In Milford, New Hampshire. You're on the air."

"Hi, Joe. How's it going?" The Joe reference was from one of the previous shows when the host used the name Joe Montana.

"It is going very well, thank you. What's up?"

Caller: "You see that story about the kid who passed for more than 200 touchdowns during his high school career?"

Announcer: "Maty Mauk. Kenton High School out in Ohio, south of Toledo—*219 passing TDs*, *18,932* total passing yards. Know who held the record *before* him?"

Caller: "No. Who?"

"His older brother, Ben."

Click. Milford sent to the bench, last of the previously recorded calls.

"Well, it has *been* fun, fans. Save your energy and questions until after Labor Day. That's when we come back."

The Rocky theme came up again.

"So, figured it out; who am I?"

The music played for 10 seconds.

"Robert Patrick 'Rocky' Bleier. Number 20. For the record, in his rookie year, he wore number 26. *Four* Super Bowl rings with the Steelers. Vietnam vet, Bronze Star, Purple Heart *and* Combat Infantryman Badge."

Music and chorus up . . . *Flyin high now.*

The theme ended, followed by three seconds of silence. A voice sounding remarkably similar to Number 20 said, "Now, stay tuned for the latest traffic update from your friend the flying squirrel . . . reporting *live* from Presque Isle, Maine."

Same night, hours later, standing at the back of Spike's Toyota pickup, AC handed out the masks. When asked by Mooko where he'd found the masks, which were obviously superior to the flimsy Halloween variety, he shook his head.

"Need to know basis. Just *wear* the fucking thing as soon as we start," AC said.

The mask he'd given Mooko looked like Kim Jong Un. He gave Moose a mask resembling Charlie Sheen; Spike got one that looked like Johnny Depp wearing glasses; and, for Whitey, the mask was Roger Stone.

AC would be wearing a wind-proof camo balaclava with an eye slit.

They examined the masks and fumbled with the elastic bands. Moose was the only one to try his on. He cocked his head playfully and got right in the face of Spike, who shoved him away.

"We go with you, dude" AC said, pointing at Mooko. "From the woods, we run across the east lot. You move the truck way up to the end and wait." He tapped his watch. "Nobody scratches their dick until 3:15. Got it? That's when we start the countdown."

Whitey nodded. They'd rehearsed this part twice back behind the Wunder Mart. Granted, the distance across the Fox Bowl lot was a longer run. But the only running Whitey needed to worry about was at the very end. At least that was the plan.

"When we come outa the stadium, we're bustin' ass to get to that warehouse up the road. Mooko's behind the wheel," Spike said.

"Right," AC said, "And he will *keep* driving. We hop in back."

After a beat, AC nodded and went on. "You go to the next spot, wait for Whitey to get there." He looked at Moose who was still wearing his Charlie Sheen mask.

"I think you can take that off for the moment," AC said. He did.

"Remember, anything goes wrong, for whatever reason, we get separated, or the speakers crap out, or the cops come sooner than I think they will, you are *on your fucking own*,"

AC said, then added: "Head for the woods to the *north*. Do not come out until after daylight and you know what you're doing."

28

WAR DRUM

"What the hell is *that*?" the security guard said.

His partner listened. A noise had started a few seconds earlier when the two men had been maybe 10 yards apart. Now they were facing each other from a distance of 10 feet.

It sounded very much like several people beating on a drum. A big drum, the kind used in a Native American Pow Wow as part of ceremonial dancing: *Pum*, pum, pum, pum. *Pum*, pum, pum, pum.

The beating grew louder and came from opposite ends of the parking area outside the stadium.

Pum, pum, pum, pum. *Pum*, pum, pum, pum. *Pum*, pum, pum, pum.

Now voices. Some form of chanting.

Both men walked in the direction of the main entrance. One guard was smiling, one was not. "Something going on in town tonight?" the smiling guard asked.

The other guard looked at his watch. "At 3:30 in the morning? I don't *think* so."

Pum, pum, pum, pum. *Pum*, pum, pum, pum.

A voice began whooping, above all the chanting and drumming.

"Better call over to Vince. Ask if they can see anything from there?" The non-smiling guard said, "I'll check the cameras."

Spike and Goose adjusted their masks. They were waiting for the signal. Only when AC was convinced that the distraction was at its peak would he let them make a run through the designated entry points. If they got that far and were able to place the dynamite where he'd told them, first major task completed. They'd gone over the drill twice in the last 24 hours.

Mooko, audio director in charge, was at the north end of the parking area, out beyond the pavement and the lights. The camo JBL Xtreme 2 bluetooth speakers were duct-taped to a cinder block in the back of the Tacoma pickup. And they were louder than the half-assed old PA speaker positioned in the rear of a Wunder Mart rent-a-truck, way over in the west side lot, Whitey behind the wheel.

As planned by AC, Mooko and Whitey, watches synched, had hit the play buttons precisely at 3:30. The sound created a cow pasture stereo effect. Maybe not up to concert standards, but pretty good.

Pum, pum, pum, pum. *Pum*, pum, pum, pum.

Three teenage boys in separate pickup trucks would be arriving next. They would rendezvous with Whitey. On his signal, five minutes after the drumming had started, each of the pickups, contracted for this special assignment from the Providence area, would head for the parking lot near the main entrance where they would make two wide circular runs.

Backward.

The kids in the trucks were told to crank up full volume the recently supplied after-market, commercial grade backup alarm systems. Assuming they avoided apprehension and in addition to $500 cash, they would get to *keep* the $26.99 Easy to Install alarms.

More than 100 yards away from the parking lot rodeo, back tight against the wall on the east side of the stadium, explosives taped around his mid-section and his eyes peering through the slit of the balaclava, AC listened and waited. *If this doesn't get us 10 minutes in and out, we're all headed for bayou country. What was that line from the song American Pie?* "They took the last train to the coast."

At precisely 3:37 a.m., turning his head first to the left, AC flashed the night vision red light on his headlamp once. Turning to his right, he repeated the procedure. He waited for a count of three, then pushed off the wall and began his quick run. In theory, all three men should be able to place the individual clusters of explosives at previously designated points.

What it would come down to at noon the next day was the effectiveness of the micro-chip initiator that AC Cahill was relying on to sequentially ignite the detonation.

Beneath all the stars and the artificial lighting, out there on that vast expanse of blacktop between U.S. Route 1 and the Fox Bowl, in the middle of the night, the drumming and chanting continued, tires were rotating and the execution of AC's "full-squad scrimmage" plan was underway.

Pum, pum, pum, pum. *Pum*, pum, pum, pum.

29

UNO, DOS

One guard was on the phone with the state police. The second guard, no longer smiling, had called the Foxborough town cops. Somebody was gonna get here flat-out quick.

The drums and chanting had now stopped. A security camera on the west side of the stadium was zooming, as close as possible, to the Wunder Mart rent-a-truck. It was parked way over behind one of the commercial buildings, no sign of anyone around.

Out near a wooded parcel and across the perimeter road to the east, red taillights flashed as a vehicle was moving. It was too far away to be certain, but one of the security guys in the video control room thought that it looked like a dark-colored pickup.

Two additional guards were leaving the stadium complex to saddle-up. They would give chase in one of the Fox Bowl security vehicles.

The teenage drivers in the pickups had completed the Demolition Derby without crashing into one another. Backup alarms now turned off, each truck sped toward Route 1; one would go north, and one would go south. The last one out of the lot could call an audible. As far as they were concerned—and they had drilled on the spiel over and over to convince AC that, if necessary, they could sell it to the cops—they would stick to the claim of "just out screwin around and meant no harm."

Pickup truck No. 3 three juked left, then went right, north on 1, the quickest route back to I-95.

Whitey sprinted past the practice fields and through the woods. Breathing hard, he pulled up his mask. No one in pursuit, no outstretched arms reaching for his jersey, no out of bounds line to worry about. No fucking refs.

His head lamp was aimed straight. He hoped that he could avoid the swamp and any fallen trees. The plan was simple: haul your ass through the woods, across the lower end of a farm pasture and get to the street. You do that, Mooko and the truck will be waiting.

Running now just as fast as he could, a tad slower than when he was in his prime, Whitey thought about AC and his back hollow boys, Spike and Moose. *Did they get in and out? Were they able to make it to the truck?*

Mooko stopped abruptly, jumped out and pulled the tonneau cover across the bed of the pickup. The speakers had been silent since he left the pavement of the east lot. Back in the cab, navigating by parking lights only, he jerked the wheel a full turn clockwise and swerved to the right. Up ahead he could see the railroad tracks and the dirt path that led behind a warehouse-distribution facility, the designated meeting spot to fetch the trio who'd taken the biggest risk of all.

It had been less than 24 hours since AC had walked everyone through the plan one last time. If they did their jobs as instructed, and the kids in the pickups held up their end, everyone would be back in the Tacoma and on their way outa here.

And there they were—AC, Spike and Moose, squatting down next to the back of a parked tractor trailer.

Mooko braked long enough for the men to jump in, all three in the back, leaving the front passenger seat empty.

Back out to Route 1 for five seconds, then a quick turn onto a side street that led through a residential neighborhood. Everyone inside the truck, except Mooko, was taking deep breaths. In the rearview mirror, Mooko could see AC's face. Balaclava stowed, he was wearing the fucking reflective mirror-blue sunglasses.

Lights off and backed into a driveway, they only had to wait a minute until Whitey came out of the woods across the street. Mooko flashed the headlights, then slowly pulled out. Whitey opened the door, got in and didn't say anything. Accelerating slowly, with only parking lights on, Mooko looked over at Whitey.

"The Bayou Flash still got it, baby," Mooko said. He looked down at Whitey's shoes and added, "Your feet ain't wet, bro. Way to hustle!"

At his very best, a long time ago in high school track, he'd run 200 meters in 21 seconds. In his football career, he'd frequently outdistanced younger players. Here in the middle of the night, slouched in the front seat of a pickup truck, he was starting to get his breathing under control, but Antoine Whitey LeBlanc, Jr. still couldn't speak.

In the back seat, Moose popped cans of Rolling Rock and passed them around. Even AC was ready for a beer. The three men had their masks turned to the back of their heads, elastic bands around their necks. Whitey's mask was missing.

"Hey, Roger. What happened to your mask?" Mooko said.

Whitey felt his head, then his neck. "Must've lost it. Fuck it."

Spike, who owned this rig, reached to the console between Mooko and Whitey, picked up his MP3 music player. He moved a finger on the center dial, then tapped a button. The truck's interior speakers, not the JBLs in the back, came to life.

A man in Tex-Mex counting: "*Uno, dos, one, two, tres, quatro.*" Then a pulsing electronic keyboard riff, guitars and a saxophone.

"Matty told Hatty, about a thing she saw. . . ."

Domingo Samudio, et al, with the classic, albeit a digital version; Sam the Sham and The Pharaohs . . . *Wooly Bully.*

30

BOOM DAY

Just 10 miles clear of the Fox Bowl, on AC's instruction from the back seat, Mooko took the next exit off the highway and a right turn at the end of the ramp. Music on the MP3 player was now some country number. Mooko had turned the volume low without complaint. He glanced in the mirror to see if his other passengers were still awake. It was 4:11 a.m.

"There's an all-night McDonald's up here a mile or so. Let's get some food," AC said. "Starvin."

"Roger that," Mooko said, then looked over at Whitey. "Where do you think you lost your mask?"

"Out in the fucking woods, of course." His defensive tone showed a slight trace of annoyance. "I was trying not to run through the fucking swamp."

"Oh-kay," Mooko said.

"You boys like to swear a lot," Moose observed. AC looked at him and studied the man's face. Leaning forward enough to see that Spike had his eyes closed and head tilted back, AC returned his focus to Moose. *Maybe he was genuinely naïve and not just dumb.*

AC said, "Moose, I'm guessing you've never served in the military."

Shauntay was wide awake. The clock showed 4:26 a.m. Jasmine was curled at the foot of the bed fast asleep.

Whitey had told her that if all went according to plan, Boom Day was imminent. Maybe that's why she had awakened so early. It was still dark, but a sliver of ambient streetlight slipped under the linen-cotton Roman window shade in the bedroom.

Normal wake-up time for Shauntay was between 7:30 and 8 most mornings. If she was alone, she would have a cup of freshly brewed green tea while she read online stories and gossip. If her man happened to be in residence, she might stay in bed until 9 o'clock or later.

As soon as the sheet was pulled back, Jasmine raised her head, ears perked and eyes alert. Shauntay gave her a love pat and went to the kitchen, the dog down onto the carpet and right behind her. Turn the burner on for the kettle then retrieve the iPad from its charger. Settling onto a wicker stool at the breakfast counter, Shauntay waited for the tablet to come alive. The first clear thought of the morning came to her. *Will there be another request for additional cash before Boom Day actually takes place?*

Whitey's secretive conduct in recent days hadn't bolstered much confidence. He'd gone mostly silent in sharing any details. But it was too late to put the brakes on. Over the past two months, a million dollars plus had been funneled via Shauntay's connection. It was with the most recent ask for another $250,000, when the clandestine funder had asked to meet Whitey *in person*.

In hindsight, possibly a mistake to have allowed that to happen. But he'd come back with the latest handoff and had assured Shauntay that that was the last trip to the well. That was a week ago. Thinking about it now, she pegged the time frame as perhaps coincidental to his current, somewhat erratic behavior.

From the outset of their now three-year relationship, Whitey had displayed a tendency to sudden mood swings and mysterious bouts of introspection. She could deal with that. It was the wandering eye and, more likely than not, the wandering penis and Shauntay's unrelenting suspicions that made all of it seem so fragile right now.

But he was still here. And he was still shelling out more than five grand a month for the condo and expenses, and another $3,000 or more a month for credit card purchases of clothing, shoes, cosmetics and incidentals.

Shauntay's modeling income was either one valley ahead or one valley beyond its peak. Either way, she didn't kid herself that she would ever make it to the top tier of the profession. And the bulk of the income she earned got salted away in a credit union account back in Asheville. She did pay for her shooting range membership. And the groceries. And most of the expenses related to Jasmine.

The tea kettle whistled. It was 4:45 a.m.

31

DAYLIGHT

Before the sun rose over the Fox Bowl, no fewer than 10 staff security guards and a mix of municipal and state police officers, in five squad cars, had thoroughly searched the area.

On foot, and slowly cruising all the parking lots, the side streets and adjacent commercial buildings, as well as the perimeter road. The hunt produced only one abandoned Wunder Mart rent-a-truck. A key left in the ignition would later be checked for prints.

Video feeds from inside and around the complex, as well as any available from nearby businesses along Route 1, would be reviewed. Somebody, somewhere, had to have something.

The cops were puzzled by a vintage, portable PA unit left in the rear of the rent-a-truck. It was connected to an old cassette tape player, cover flipped open but no cassette.

One security guard thought that the drumming they'd heard might have been recorded.

A little after daybreak, Jack the Cabbie pulled into the usual parking spot a short walk from his tower. Surprised to see local police cars and a Mass. State Police SUV near the main entrance, he hesitated.

Something goin' on out there I don't know about? Where on earth is Trooper Julie?

Phone calls and numerous text messages were flying. Lots of speculation, more than a little confusion, and no small amount of frustration. It all had gone down in less than 15 minutes, in the middle of the night, and for *what*?

No apparent vandalism, no graffiti, no injuries.

The two security guards who first sent the balloon up were pretty sure that the yahoos driving backward in the pickup trucks looked like kids.

Lieutenant Frank Sullivan was one of the state cops called to the scene and was not particularly happy to be out this early in the morning. When he saw Jack the Cabbie shuffling toward his stupid tower setup, Sullivan headed in the same direction.

"Hey, Jack. Hang on a minute," Sullivan said.

One hand reaching up and a foot on the second rung of the ladder, Jack stopped.

"And a fine day to you boys wearing the blue and the gray," Jack said, offering a pretend salute. "Might I enquire about the intrepid Trooper Julie. Where would she be on such a lovely morning?"

Sullivan: "Just what I was about to ask you."

Jack: "Ah, but you see, Lieutenant, Trooper Egan and I have much in common, including an appreciation for good food, drink and a story or two. Alas, she does not keep me apprised of her every move."

Sullivan slowly scanned the lot where Jack's cab was parked. No other vehicles were anywhere near his.

Jack: "It was my very distinct impression that, although Trooper Egan is simply on loan to your headquarters, that she does, in fact, report directly to you. Might I be correct on that?"

Sullivan wanted to smack the fucker. Sure, he was a "valued asset" for an ongoing investigation. And, yes, Sullivan knew all about Jack's quirkiness. But *smugness* from anyone, let alone at the start of the day, was not Frank Sullivan's idea of how to maintain good rapport. Plus, the fact that Sullivan had been pondering a strong hunch about the nature of the relationship between Trooper Julie and Cabbie Jack.

"How about a cup of coffee?" Sullivan said. "My treat."

Jack studied the Lieutenant. He wondered if he had his uniform tailored. Sullivan pointed at his SUV. "Red Wing's not open yet. We'll have to run up street to Dunkin. I'll bring you back here."

"Very considerate," Jack said. "But I'll follow you. Don't want to impose." *And sure as shit don't want to ride anytime soon in another Mass. State Police vehicle.*

Julie Egan had been up half the night putting the finishing touches on her report for a Homeland Security Division meeting scheduled for the next morning in Framingham.

Aside from information she'd gleaned from a variety of sources, primarily Cabbie Jack, Egan was not convinced there was a real threat to public safety coming from "individuals, organizations or groups" outside the Commonwealth of Massachusetts. On the other hand, and this is where it got fuzzy, Trooper Egan had serious doubts about calling it a wrap just quite yet. There was pressure from Colonel Ronald McCune, or so she believed, to tie things up, finish her assignment out there in "pigskin pasture" and get on to other work. A budget was a budget and McKune had no interest in boondoggles of any sort.

What Egan believed, though she lacked sufficient evidence at the moment, was there really was *someone*—possibly more than one person— who was up to something and that the Fox Bowl was involved. If asked to justify her suspicions on short notice, without further investigation, it came down to the yellow Corvette. What she'd earlier chalked up as coincidence at seeing a car on three different occasions and not having bothered to run the vehicle's description, it was the license plate that stuck in her mind.

Some football crazy? Maybe. An offshore sport fisherman? Possibly.

Picking a Sumatra reserve dark roast from her selection of coffees, Egan poured a mug of water into the machine, put the single-cup pod in place, closed the lid and pressed the button.

Seconds later, the shower running full spray, Trooper Julie did not hear her phone in the next room.

Sullivan was already in a booth inside the Dunkin Donuts when Jack came through the door. The lieutenant was putting his cellphone away as Jack started to take a seat.

"Get me an original blend," Sullivan said, handing a $10 bill to Jack.

"Cream, sugar?"

"Black. Large."

Cabbie Jack was not accustomed to taking brusque orders. *But, hey. This guy is in charge, or so says Trooper Julie. What the hell?*

When he returned with two cups of coffee and handed the change to Sullivan, Jack hesitated before taking a seat, as though he was expecting some other command.

Sullivan removed the lid from his coffee, blew on it and took sip. Jack placed his own coffee on the table and lowered himself into the booth.

"Let's not beat around the bush, here, Jack. I know you have a sweet deal on the suspended sentence and that you're helping with that Russian asshole who ran the limo scam," Sullivan said.

"Of course, you know that. And though we did not discuss such matters when we first met back in the winter, I suspect that you know quite a bit more about yours truly. Correcto?"

"That would be affirmative," Sullivan said, waving his hand in dismissal. "But what I really need to ascertain. . . ."

Jack laughed before Sullivan could finish. "Great word. Ascertain." Jack took a sip of his coffee. Sullivan waited to see if the man had more to say. Apparently not.

"Let me get right to it, okay? You would not be, uh, shall we say, *compromising* Trooper Egan in any of her duties, would you?"

Jack locked eyes with Sullivan. Neither man spoke, though Sullivan displayed what could only be called a sneer. After a long five seconds or so, Jack sat back and raised an arm to rest on the back of the booth. He swiveled his head slowly, like maybe he'd been asked for an opinion on the lighting. Finally bringing his focus back to Sullivan, Jack smiled. Sullivan waited.

"Perhaps to put this in proper perspective, allow me to quote an old and wise Scottish gamekeeper. Fuck off."

Jack stood, picked up his cup and smiled at Sullivan. "Thanks for the coffee." With that, he was headed out the door and Lieutenant Frank Sullivan was no more enlightened than he'd been an hour earlier. But he did have a pretty good idea about who might be compromising whom.

32

WATCH THE NEWS

The Boom Plan was rapidly approaching the crucial point, only hours remaining. With the dynamite and C-4 in place, the final step would be the use of a laser detonator to trigger the explosives.

During one of Whitey's multiple visits to the "expert's bunker" out back behind the Wunder Mart, after handing over still another bag of cash, AC had gone on at length about the different properties of explosives, detonation velocity, blast wave propagation and a bunch of details that might make the average bear want to stay in his den.

Whitey was never sure whether AC launched into these soliloquies as an attempt to impress him and justify the money, or if he was one of those guys who simply couldn't help himself once he got started, *irrespective* of how much the listener might actually comprehend.

Both Whitey and Mooko, however, were easily convinced by the expert's mantra: if you wanna blow it up, *placement and charge preparation* are key. So, it really didn't matter that the guy might be a little strange. For better or for worse, at a price tag even higher than The Mayor had first suggested, here they were.

AC had done all the work: research, planning, obtaining materials from a Rhode Island source, then instructing and managing his small group of helpers. Now it would be a solo mission, AC driving his 20-year-old wreck of a car in broad daylight, right smack through the Fox Bowl parking lots, to put the laser icing on the cake.

Boom. And boom again. They hoped.

Following their pre-dawn breakfast sandwiches, burritos, hotcakes, coffee and two little jugs of fat-free chocolate milk, Spike was behind the wheel of the pickup, Moose riding shotgun, Whitey, Mooko and AC now in the back seat. It was 5:22 a.m.

The sun wouldn't clear the horizon for another 15 minutes. They dropped AC off near a wooded area half a mile from the Wunder Mart. He would make his way home to get some sleep before the "big drive." Whitey had left the Corvette parked behind the motel where Spike and Moose were staying. He and Mooko would go back to his condo in Quincy.

And wait.

Michael O'Connolly had long ago learned to follow two adages in life. First, the best business deal you do is often the one you don't. Second, what you don't know can often save your sorry ass—what the defense lawyers called "plausible deniability."

So, when he told a certain hyped-up, caffeine-charged former wide receiver that he didn't want to know the date or even the time of Boom Day, he really meant it.

Keep your goddamn gossipy chitchat to yourself. I've done my part. Go carry out your preposterous scheme. Leave me out of the culminating drama. Sweet Jesus, Mary and Joseph, let a working man drink in peace.

He had disciplined himself to gaze momentarily and shake it off. Move on mentally. Still, he couldn't help but sometimes wonder.

The Mayor of Somerville was happily ensconced in his new office at the Hilltop, now in room No. 17, loading his Henry classic lever-action rifle ("Made in America and Priced Right!") with 15 rounds of .22 longs.

He had moved the queen bed away from the wall, revealing years of fuzzy gray grime peppered with a minefield of used condoms, positioning himself with a clear view out the open door. He was leaning back against the flimsy headboard on a couple of stained pillows, beside him a giant brightly colored half-empty bag of Lays potato chips.

O'Connolly was peering down the 18½-inch blued barrel, through old-fashioned open sights. He considered them more sporting than a scope. He was aiming across the seedy parking lot toward the battered steel guardrails on the other side of the highway. He'd have to time his shot between the streaming trucks and delivery vans whizzing by.

He was about to squeeze the trigger—steady, exhale Mikey, steady—on a fat Norway rat the size of a house cat, when his cellphone jumped to life. He shifted his eyes enough to see the caller ID. It was Whitey.

Goddamn it!

"What now?"

"Watch the news."

33

JUST ANOTHER DAY

When she arrived later at State Police General Headquarters in Framingham, Trooper Julie Egan was prepared. She'd thought about, rehearsed, and thought some more. It was one notch closer to a plausible theory. Something else was going on out at the Fox Bowl.

Sure, Jack the Cabbie had been useful, not to mention entertaining, but he had dropped the ball when it came to identifying any real bad actors or suspects warranting the attention of the Massachusetts State Police Homeland Security Division.

Maybe Hackie Jack had cast one too many flies over the years. Maybe it all had become just one big hoot to him. Pass the flask, let's party and read esoteric fiction. But Trooper Egan could feel it. More was at play than he realized.

Colonel McCune wouldn't pull her today. Too much time and money had been invested and, at a minimum, she'd developed a bond with Lieutenant McCormack and the officers at the Foxboro barracks. Perhaps a good idea to leave her out there through the end of the year. Who knows what could happen?

Egan got out of her car and went through a side entrance of the HQ. This meeting should end by 10 o'clock. She would say her piece, answer questions and be back on the road by 10:30. Twenty miles south, she could be in Foxborough 40 minutes after she left Framingham.

Approaching Colonel McCune's office, she had a new thought about the yellow corvette: *go to the Red Wing and talk to Dave behind the bar. He knows everybody.*

Things appeared to be returning to normal at the Fox Bowl when employees began arriving for work a little before 9. Day shift security guards had already checked in and were briefed about the middle of the night shenanigans. Only two municipal cops were still on the scene reviewing video with one of the overnight guards.

"That's a Rhode Island plate on the front of the blue pickup," a security guard observed. "I'm sure of it." The angle wasn't great, but the others agreed that it certainly appeared to be the blue, gray and white plate from the Ocean State.

All three of the trucks had covered their rear license plate with plastic bags.

Doors wouldn't open to the general public until 10 o'clock. From all appearances, it should be another normal day of pre-season fan enthusiasm and brisk cash register activity.

Jack the Cabbie was back in his tower wrapping feathers on a hook while sipping the remnants of a cold cup of coffee which he spiked with a couple ounces of Remy Martin cognac.

Out in the parking lot, it looked like another day on the water. Only problem being that the water was all fucking blacktop, concrete and granite. And a bunch of towering light poles. But Jack could get in the zone as well as any record-setting, Hall of Fame football player.

While it might be the thrill of the crowd noise and the vibrations of pounding feet chasing you down the artificial turf that did it for some, for Jack, it was the meticulous wrap of the thread and the correct selection and placement of a rooster feather that sucked him into a euphoric trance.

He didn't need any blinders. However, the vintage Radio Shack headband-over-ear headphones did help.

Where the hell is Trooper Julie?

34

IT'S ALL RELATIVE

AC Cahill sat bolt upright. Eyes wide open, the interior of the shipping container was dark and silent. He listened hard, not moving a muscle. Eyes shifting left, right, up, down. Nothing.

He took a deep breath through his nose, held it for 10 seconds, then blew out through his mouth. Relaxing his shoulder muscles, he rotated his neck, swung both legs off the bunk and placed bare feet on the cold metal floor. It was a dream. People were running and shouting. There was a man standing near the woods wearing the Roger Stone mask. *Fuck.*

AC rubbed his eyes, yawned and got up slowly. He looked at his G-Shock digital wristwatch on the plastic crate next to the bunk: SAT 8-24 8:52:30. He'd been asleep just shy of three hours.

Reaching for his phone, he moved carefully toward the door and pushed it open with his left foot. He stepped back from the bright light and looked around for his sunglasses.

The number rang three times.

"Thought we said 10 o'clock," Whitey said, sounding groggy and surprised by the call more than an hour ahead of schedule.

"Adjustment to the plan. Get here quick as you can. Bring your man Spike and his truck. I'll be out by my car. ASAP, dude."

The connection was broken. Whitey stared at his phone.

Mooko was still asleep on the fold-out sofa. In all likelihood, Spike and Moose were also still asleep at the motel one block away.

It was 9:45 when Whitey and the crew arrived at the Wunder Mart parking lot. Spike knew where to go from previous trips, down behind the rent-a-trucks where AC kept his beat-up old Honda Civic. One tire smaller than the others. No hub caps. Cracked rear window. Dash littered with unopened bills and unpaid parking tickets.

And there he was, camo shorts, T-shirt, running shoes

and no socks. Mirror sunglasses in place. He rested his ass on the hood of the car next to a camo backpack. He watched as they approached.

Whitey was riding shotgun and buzzed the window down. "Hey, what's up?" he said. The two big guys in the crew, Mooko and Moose, were taking up a lotta room in the back seat.

"Can't happen. Not the way I planned it," AC said. "Gotta make a change."

"*What*?" Whitey said, voice rising in astonishment.

AC took a step closer to the truck, pushed his sunglasses up on his forehead and rubbed a big right hand across his mouth as though he were wiping away chocolate milk.

"Can't happen? What are you talking about?" Whitey said, opening the door of the truck to get out.

AC stopped rubbing his mouth, folded his arms and glared directly at Whitey. He offered up a menacing smile. "Want your money back?"

"Fuck, no, man. We gotta *do* this," Whitey said.

AC held the smile. They were standing two feet apart. Whitey extended both his arms, hands out, palms up.

"*What* change? What're you *talking* about?"

AC did the deep breath through the nose routine and rubbed his mouth again. "We're gonna add a sub, AC said.

"Need one more player to go along with us. Part of the distraction I overlooked."

The "sub" AC had in mind was an old guy who lived in the village. He instructed Whitey and Mooko to stay with him and he sent Spike and Moose off to find the man.

"Drive around until you spot him. Skinny guy riding an old bicycle. Coupla mesh bags tied to the rear fender, like saddle bags. White plastic storage crate fastened to the handlebars. Wears a faded plaid shirt buttoned to the neck. And an old farmer's hat with ear flaps tied up on top."

Spike stared at AC as though he was putting him on.

"Give him this," AC said, handing Spike a $100 bill. "Tell him to come find AC, right now. Urgent—I need some help." AC added, "His name's Einstein."

"C'mon, man," Spike said.

"That's his name, dude. Trust me. Give him the money. Tell him no time to waste."

Spike put the $100 bill above his sun visor and slowly pulled away, leaving AC, Whitey and Mooko standing next to AC's heap.

Not 20 minutes after they left, Spike and Moose were back. AC had been holding forth on the adjustment to the plan. The explanation made sense and, with encouragement from Mooko, Whitey had settled down.

"He's on his way," Spike said. "I could see him in my rearview out on the highway." Spike laughed and added, "Pedaling like it's the Tour de France."

"Good," AC said. He looked at Mooko and AC. "You guys go get coffee. Meet me back here at," he looked at his watch, "11:45. Don't be late."

The "taxi squad" was back inside Spike's pickup and off they went.

AC headed for his shipping container. He had just over an hour before everybody would be on the road for an encore appearance at the Fox Bowl.

When Einstein showed up on his vintage bicycle with fat tires, the mesh bags tied to the rear were half full of empty soda cans and plastic bottles. He leaned the bike against the side of the shipping container and banged on the door.

"AC—you in there?" He knocked again. "You okay?"

The door opened. Not only did AC appear to be all right, he had a big grin on his face and a fist full of $100 bills.

"Thanks for coming, Plute. Come on in. We gotta hurry here," AC said.

"Plute" was short for plutonium. There was probably someone around who knew this guy's real name, but AC, and as far as he knew everyone within 20 miles, knew the man only as Einstein Plutonium.

If anyone had done any research, they weren't talking about it.

"Have a seat," AC said, gesturing to the taped-up plastic visitor's chair. "Here. This is for you," he added, handing more $100 bills to the man, who shoved the cash into his shirt pocket and sat as instructed.

"Now listen careful, man. I can only go through this once."

For 10 minutes, AC slowly outlined what was about to happen and what he needed Einstein Plutonium to do. Despite what he'd said at the beginning, AC repeated the key points and watched to be sure that Plute was getting it. The man nodded.

"I'm gonna have to do a little moulage work on you," AC said. "No worry. It'll wash off with soap and water."

AC retrieved a plastic container that looked like a medium-sized tackle box. He removed a small round container, twisted off the lid to expose a powder-blue paste. Taking a tiny sponge from the box, he dabbed the paste.

"Tilt your head back," he said. Plute did as he was told. AC applied the blue paste above the man's upper lip, with just a smidge actually on his lips, then applied more liberal amounts to the back of his hands and fingers. He rubbed it in as though he was applying sunscreen.

The old man grinned through two cracked yellow teeth.

Just up the road, on the other side of U.S. Route 1, Trooper Julie Egan had stopped at the Red Wing. She wasn't sure if Dave would be on duty, but she was eager to pump him for info on the yellow Corvette and the two men she'd seen at the diner earlier.

Turned out that Dave didn't have names, but he confirmed that they had been there numerous times. He said the guy who drove the 'vette, the one with a diamond stud in his left ear and wearing a gold neck chain, had also stopped in by himself a couple of times.

As soon as Julie got back to her cruiser, she ran a check on the license plate. The car was owned and registered to an LLC, Bayou Business Enterprises, with an address on Washington Street in Quincy.

AC stood back and looked at his makeup job on Plute, checking his face, then both hands. *That'll work.*

"Great. Now hustle back and stash the money, then head straight to the Fox Bowl. We'll find you in the parking lot and I'll give you the signal."

Einstein Plutonium was back on his bicycle and pedaling away from the Wunder Mart, more like he was going for the yellow jersey in the Tour de Walpole.

35

RUN!

Back to the plan as originally scripted by AC, all five men were once again in Spike's pickup and on their way to the Fox Bowl. Spike and Moose up front, Whitey, Mooko and AC in the back.

Late morning and the usual amount of traffic on Route 1. Not heavy, not slow, no accidents, moving right along at a normal pace.

None of the men spoke. AC, dressed in the suit and wearing the Marv Albert hairpiece once more, had the reflective sunglasses on and his earbuds in. Only he knew what he was listening to. Spike slowed as they got closer to the turnoff.

At the far end of the northern most parking area, there was Einstein Plutonium standing astride his vintage bicycle.

Spike saw the old man and swiveled his head enough to see AC in the back seat. AC nodded.

Then, like a ref indicating first down, AC shot out his arm and pointed in the direction of the old guy on the bike. Mooko and Whitey looked in that direction. They were somewhat at a disadvantage as AC had not thoroughly briefed them on precisely what role the old man would play, other than another distraction.

The pickup stopped two yards short of the man and the bike. Only AC got out. He walked over and put a hand on Plute's shoulder.

"We all set?" he said.

The old man looked at him, wet his lips, smiled and said, "I am enough of an artist to draw freely upon my imagination."

AC also smiled and patted the man's shoulder. "Okay, friend. Just as soon as you see this truck going back out to the highway, *that* is your cue. Give em hell."

Once AC had climbed into the pickup, Spike backed around and off they went. A minute later they were at the southeast corner of the parking lot and AC got out again.

"Wait here for five minutes," he said, tapping his wristwatch. Spike looked at the clock on the dashboard and gestured with a thumb up. Whitey looked at his Rolex, Mooko checked his Movado, Moose was watching a small crowd of pedestrians near the front entrance of the complex.

"As soon as I'm out of sight, *go*. Next time you see me will be out in the neighborhood. Don't fuck it up now, gentlemen." AC walked off in the direction of the stadium.

At 1:25 p.m, with approximately 40 people either entering or leaving the main building at the Fox Bowl, and perhaps another 75 to 100 inside, a man on a bicycle came pedaling casually through the parking area closest to the front entrance.

The man stopped and got off the bike. He knelt to check the chain and tugged on it as though he were trying to tighten it. That's when the first security guard began watching the man. Apparently satisfied that his chain was okay, the man stood, straddled the seat and put his right foot on a pedal ready to push off. And that's when he started shouting.

"BOMB!" he yelled. "There are explosives inside the stadium. BOMB!"

He began pedaling away. People turned to watch the old man. He was circling in a loop, maybe 15 yards from the person closest to him.

"Run! The place is going to *explode*."

And people did run. In different directions, toward the parking lot, toward nearby buildings not attached to the Fox Bowl. A woman began screaming. Then other voices joined in. Small scale mayhem on a hot, late summer afternoon.

Up in his camouflage tower, listening to the Boston Public Radio show on WGBH, Jack the Cabbie stuck his head out to see what all the yelling was about. He watched the man circling on the bicycle and knew immediately that it was Einstein Plutonium, the local bum who fetched returnable bottles and cans from the side of the road.

"Einstein. *What the hell* is all the excitement?" Jack shouted down.

The old man looked up at the tower. Raising his right arm and nearly falling off the bike, he waved in a "get away" motion to Jack: "BOMB. The place is going to explode!"

At that moment, two Fox Bowl guards were on the old man and wrestled him to the ground.

"Oh, shit," one of the guards said. "I think he's having a heart attack."

The old man had grabbed at his chest, his eyes bugged wide and he let out a moan. "Bomb," he managed to sputter out one last time.

"Nah. He's going into shock," the guard said. "Look at his hands."

The man's hands were trembling and had bluish tint.

"Call an ambulance," said the guard bending over the old man. The front wheel of the bike was still spinning. People were still running. Jack the Cabbie was descending the ladder.

Following the early morning false alarm at the Fox Bowl and an unsatisfactory few minutes in the company of Jack the Cabbie, Lieutenant Frank Sullivan had spent two tedious hours back in his office.

Now, eager for some down time, Sullivan decided to pack it in early. The Sox were on tonight and he was looking forward to a little time with his eight-year-old granddaughter.

He picked up the phone and dialed the Red Wing. Get an order of crab cakes and a clam basket to go. A cold bottle of Harpoon, a shower, and park his carcass in front of the big screen. None of that "Breaking News" nonsense on his TV tonight. If those posturing clowns can't make government work, they would not get *one single minute* of his attention this weekend.

The desk phone buzzed. He looked at it a second before picking up the receiver. "Sullivan."

"Lieutenant. We have an incident at the Fox Bowl. A man is reporting a bomb inside the stadium," came the reply from a HQ dispatcher.

Inside the main building guards were instructing staff and patrons to evacuate. Most of it appeared to be under control with orderly, quick compliance.

There was one exception. A middle-aged woman came out of the second-floor restroom and saw everyone moving toward the exits. She called to her husband who was standing next to the down escalator.

"Herman. What's wrong? Is it a fire drill?"

Wavy bleach-blonde hair, prominent chin, maybe 60 years old, the husband looked like a human version of Dudley Do-Right, minus the RCMP hat and red coat. This guy, Herman, was wearing a Miami Dolphins cap, a nautical aqua-and-orange striped shirt over khaki pants and Velcro-closure white sneakers.

"There appears to be a bomb," Herman said, with just a twinge of a smile. His wife looked at the crowd downstairs moving through the doors, then back to her husband. He was not kidding.

"Are the TV people here?" she said. "How's my hair," she added, fluffing the gray strands on both sides of her head. She turned and went back into the restroom.

Herman was still waiting when a female security guard told him that he would have to go outside. Now.

"My wife's in the bathroom," he said, smiling.

"Go," the guard said emphatically, pointing to the lower level. "I will round up your wife."

At a counter near one of the registers in the gift and souvenir shop, a young woman was in the middle of wrapping the full collection of player bobbleheads. She'd been at it for 15 minutes. The customer had already paid and wanted the package shipped immediately.

"Kaitlyn. Let's go," a supervisor said.

"I'm almost finished."

The supervisor took Kaitlyn firmly by the arm and said, "Those can wait. Let's *go*."

A bobblehead of one of the Pirates offensive lineman from the '80s, Josh Hanner, bounced happily on the counter unaware of who else was already in the box and just where they were being shipped.

The old man on the bicycle was breathing normally, no longer clutching his chest. The security guards had allowed him to sit up, ass on the pavement and leaning forward with arms resting on his knees. But he was still a little blue around the gills. And his hands and fingers.

Most of the crowd had been cleared from near the front entrance and people were still coming out of the main building. Employees and shoppers from adjacent buildings began to appear on the sidewalk.

"How do you know there is a bomb?" one of the guards asked the old man.

He began to sway, head, shoulders, all of his upper body, moving more like a rocking bobble-head. Rhythmically from side to side, moving only above the waist while keeping his arms on his knees.

But the old man didn't say a word.

Kneeling down and lightly placing a hand on the man's right foot, the guard pressed for information. "Who told you there's a bomb?"

"You live in town, don't you?" said the second guard, standing above the man. "What's your name?"

The old man kept up the swaying, but now he looked over at the second guard and *maybe* gave a faint smile.

And then, off in the distance, the sound of an explosion.

Boom.

Muffled, distant. like it was miles away.

A second subdued boom. Maybe closer.

There was some screaming from the parking lot crowd, even though there hadn't been the slightest vibration from the nearby pavement. No shattering glass, no flying concrete, no desks, chairs or footballs being launched from inside the hulking edifice.

Just two little booms.

36

THIS DOESN'T LOOK RIGHT

A total of eight state police vehicles arrived within minutes of the first call. When Sullivan got there, a bomb squad unit out of the Fire and Explosion Investigation Section was already on the scene.

A matched pair of bomb-sniffing dogs, Rolfe and Rudy, were already engaged at the main entrance, part of the nationally certified canine teams assigned to the Massachusetts State Police.

A couple of staff security guards at the complex had cornered the unarmed elderly man in the front parking lot. He appeared to be in shock and was now being treated by EMTs from the Town of Foxborough Fire-Emergency Services

Department. They had the old man on a gurney and were about to transport him to a nearby Health Center not more than 200 yards away.

WTF? thought AC. None of the dynamite had exploded and only two of the small packets of the C-4 seemed to have worked, one outside the home team locker room and one under the Press Box.

AC himself might actually be going into shock. He couldn't chance hanging around, cops and security staff would be everywhere.

Peeling off the suit, shirt, clip-on tie and the hairpiece, he stuffed all of it into a large trash receptacle stamped with the Pirates logo. He held onto the laser detonator. Back to the camo shorts and a T-shirt he wore underneath the suit, he pulled flip-flops from a cargo pocket, slipped them on and kept moving.

Walking briskly to the far parking area away from the main entrance, AC hoped that he would look like anyone else circulating in the retail-service area near the stadium. But he was going to have to improvise. He couldn't chance running toward the woods and out to the designated pick up spot. So, he took his time on one of the divider streets, stopping to read a menu in the window of a restaurant.

Multiple sirens and people noise could be heard not a block from where he stood. The best move now would be to walk at a normal pace and hope to get close enough to the residential neighborhood where the others would be waiting. They would see him.

Music in the truck at low volume was Dr. Dre and Snoop Dogg. It was uncertain if all four men were listening, but all four of them were being quiet. Only Moose, in the front passenger seat, was moving his head and shoulders with the groove.

"There he is," Spike said, starting the engine.

"What the fuck's he doing coming that way?" Whitey said. He looked at Mooko, then added, "you hear anything after that first little explosion?"

Mooko shook his head.

"Something's not right."

AC was walking toward them as though he was just out in the neighborhood searching for a lost cat.

"Wait," Whitey said, putting a hand on Spike's shoulder. "Don't pull out. Let him get here. Make sure nobody's on him."

At the pace AC was walking, it could be another five minutes.

Mooko said, "Nah. Something *wrong* with this picture."

Shauntay had convinced herself that Whitey really was working on The Plan and not out chasing girls. Still, she had doubts.

He was not spending as much time at her condo as he had in the spring and early summer. But, on four occasions, she had arranged for the transfer of cash to support the Boom Project, and each time Whitey came to get the money he was on his best behavior. No fights, good sack time and, he was still covering the bulk of her living expenses, excluding the monthly lease payments on her SUV.

No requests for additional funds in more than a week now. In fact, no talk at all about money since Whitey had the one-on-one meeting with the investor.

Maybe she'd shut off the cash and he didn't have the nerve to tell me?

"Probably," she said to Jasmine, who didn't respond. Which made Shauntay recall her mother's take on all probabilities being 50-50; it either will or will not happen.

Time for some personal attention; she had an appointment to keep. Jasmine was good for the afternoon. Placing her phone in the shoulder bag, Shauntay left the condo.

37

RECALIBRATING

The med techs had taken the old man to get him checked out. Other than *possibly* being in shock, he did not appear to be injured or suffering from any medical emergency. But the man wasn't talking. Sullivan asked one of the town cops, *not* under his command, if he could stay with the guy while he was being treated.

"Sure," the cop said. "But I gotta tell you, Lieutenant, this is *one* strange character. He's been around town for a few years and is a real loner. Uses a bullshit fake name."

"We'll sort that out later. Just stay with him. Don't let 'em release the guy until one of my troopers shows up."

And a number of those troopers were still gathered out front, while the private security staff employed by the team was working inside the complex. Other municipal cops were practicing their skills at crowd and traffic control, even with a smaller than normal crowd that one might expect to see leaving the Fox Bowl.

No one was allowed to enter the main building or the stadium. The bomb squad and the dogs were inside somewhere.

AC slipped into the back seat next to Whitey. Nobody said a word. The engine was idling, but Spike waited for a signal to pull out.

"What's going on?" Whitey asked. "We didn't hear nothin. Just one little poof."

AC said, "There were two."

"We only heard one," Whitey repeated.

AC turned and looked at him. "There were *two*," he said, holding up two fingers in Whitey's face. "Two. Five seconds apart, just like I planned it."

"Okay. More gonna go when we leave?"

"Highly fucking unlikely," AC said. "Let's go—what're you waiting for?"

Spike lifted his hands off the steering wheel and looked over his shoulder to the back seat. "Where to?" he asked.

"Head north, back out to 95. Take your time through this neighborhood. Don't need any extra attention now," AC said.

The truck eased forward slowly. Even if someone was looking at the rig, they were not going to see three guys in the back. The solar-eclipse tinting on the side windows made it next to impossible to see inside. Of course, there was the chance that someone had seen the extended-cab Toyota parked there, waiting, and had then seen AC walk up and get in the back. Less of a chance that anyone would've seen it earlier, in the middle of the night when the explosives had been placed.

In a time-killing, circuitous route first north on I-95, off the highway and half way around the cloverleaf, immediately back on and heading south, Spike followed directions from the back seat as though AC was auditioning for a GPS gig. "Take the next left. Get off in six miles, Exit 9."

Despite clear agitation from Whitey and a question or two from Mooko, AC had shut it down.

"Not now," he'd told them. "I gotta think about this."

It wasn't clear if they were intimidated by AC, or, maybe like him, stuck somewhere between disbelief and tongue-tied confusion. What had gone wrong with multiple explosives carefully, but hastily, placed inside the Fox Bowl the night before?

Didn't matter. Not now. He was the professional, they had followed every step he had laid out and, as frustrating as it might be for the moment, *he* was still in charge. So, everyone kept their mouths shut.

Spike flipped on his turn signal for the exit ramp. As they got closer to the Wunder Mart, AC leaned forward and said, "Same spot you dropped me before. Loop around and I'll get out."

Spike nodded, his eyes on the rearview mirror glancing to Whitey, who saw the look but said nothing.

"The material we got from O'Connolly's guy was *crap*. Looked right, but didn't fucking work," AC said. Whitey was all ears.

"I'm gonna make some calls, maybe have to go see someone. Find out who shit in the sink here. These assholes don't know who their dealin with," AC added.

Spike stopped the truck for AC to get out. The front of the Wunder Mart lot, half a football field away, was filling up with cars and a couple of RVs at the far end. Standing on the blacktop, camo shorts, flip flops, T-shirt and the mirror sunglasses, much like the first time Whitey laid eyes on him, AC did not give off a vibe inviting more discussion.

"Keep your phone on. You'll hear from me," AC said as he turned away from the truck.

The Mayor *was* surprised to get a call from AC Cahill. He'd watched the news as Whitey had told him to do. There had been nothing. Now, the middle of the afternoon, here's another phone call, this time from the main guy.

"Listen carefully," AC said. "I want you to get your pathetic ass in that fucking antique shit bucket you drive and meet me out front in one hour."

"Hold on. Out fronta *where*?" O'Connolly said.

"Out front of Symphony Hall. I'll be the one with white roses, asshole. Meet me out front of the Wunder-fucking-Mart, dipshit. You know where *that is*, right?"

"Wait a second. . . ." AC cut him off.

"No wait a second. *One . . . hour.* You and I need to take a little road trip. Your guy who sold me the 'supplies' has some explaining to do. A lot of fucking money got thrown around here for something that did not go as planned, know what I mean?"

The call ended. On his TV, now there was a woman reporter standing in front of what looked like a perfectly intact Fox Bowl. The Mayor picked up the remote to punch up the volume.

38

BEING A GOOD CITIZEN

The reporter on TV wrapped up her live report with the words "the Massachusetts State Police Homeland Security Division and the FBI will continue the investigation. *What* really happened here, and *who* might be responsible, is still a mystery."

It took The Mayor all of 10 seconds to realize what he needed to do. He picked up the phone and speed-dialed a friend.

"Hey, Tommy. It's Mikey," he said. "Listen. How close are you to this AC Cahill?"

"We know each other. You know, I know his family. I saw him a lot as a kid, knew about his time in the Army. He came back a little weird. Why, you got another job for him?"

"No, no. I put him touch with somebody else coupla months back. You know, I told you about it," O'Connolly said. "Turns out maybe things didn't work out so well."

"Yeah? That's too bad. But it happens, right?"

"Cops may be after AC," O'Connolly added. Tommy didn't reply.

Even though O'Connolly had, in fact, previously mentioned to his friend that he'd been successful in connecting AC and another man on a "project," he did not burden Tommy with details, including information about the cool 10 large that The Mayor had skimmed for being the "facilitator."

"Possible he's gonna get nailed by the feds," O'Connolly said.

"Tough break," Tommy said.

"He's not the kinda guy who snitches on his pals, is he?"

"Hey," Tommy said. "Got me there. I wouldn't think so. I mean, we all got pals, right.? Don't wanna it to get around that you talk too much, huh?"

"You're exactly right, Tommy. I wouldn't think so. I owe you."

Putting the phone down, The Mayor thought, *The crazy shit better keep his mouth shut.* He sat back on the bed and considered human nature. But he didn't have to consider it for long.

Frowning, O'Connolly got up, went over to an old mason's canvas satchel in the closet, rummaged around and pulled out a cheap, disposable cellphone with no traceable number.

"Good afternoon," said a woman's voice, "Massachusetts State Police, Foxborough Barracks."

A gruff, gravelly voice said, "I gotta tip."

Thirty minutes with weights, a quart of his own home-brew sports drink to keep his body in balance, a quick hosing under the makeshift inside Sun Shower, and AC was toweling off when he heard the helicopter outside. He pushed the shipping container door open and the thumping of the chopper's blades immediately grew louder.

It was a six-seater AS355 Practical Eurocopter manufactured in France that sold for a tidy $3.6 million to the U. S. market under the name Twin Star. This one-of-five turbine machines operated by the Mass. State Police Helicopter Air Wing—the largest public emergency aviation unit in New England on 24-hour standby—had been dispatched from Air Base Lawrence. The pilots were on alert for a potential hostage situation.

The chopper was directly overhead. AC stuck his head out. That's when he heard the voice from a bullhorn: "State Police. Come out with your hands over your head."

Glaring into the late-afternoon sun, AC put a hand over his brow, much like Coach Willy often does, then stepped back from the door.

"Give me a minute," he shouted back.

"Come out *now*! Hands over your head."

What the hell. It's only gonna get worse.

AC took a deep breath, rolled his neck and shoulders, picked up his sunglasses and put them on, then cinched the large, faded Garfield cartoon beach towel around his waist.

Stepping slowly from the orange shipping container decorated with the giant Aquaman decal, he raised both hands high above his head in an imitation of a boxer declaring victory. He did not dance, shuffle, bob or weave. There were police cars all over the place, flashing blue lights. He could see at least two scoped rifles aimed in his direction. He guessed they were M24 U. S. Army sniper systems.

The M24 is based on the commercial Remington 700 hunting rifle and chambered in .308 Winchester/7.62x51mm NATO, he heard a voice echoing from his sergeant back in Kabul. *Features a custom-made 24-inch free-floating barrel with a Leupold Mark IV M3 fixed 10X scope.*

AC stood perfectly still, shifting his eyes slowly left to right behind the sunglasses. *How the fuck did this happen?*

39

LOOKY LOOS

Out in the front parking lot of the Super Wunder Mart, the view from the Twin Star helicopter hovering overhead was of borderline pandemonium.

Route 1 and all the approach roads were jammed with growing throngs of looky loos—"civilians," as AC thought of them—a gathering horde riled up by Facebook and Instagram and a frenzy of texts that something big was going down at the Walpole Wunder Mart. They jumped in their cars and trucks and put their navigational faith in the GPS gods.

The great race was on. When everything jammed up, some people stopped and got out for a smoke break or to take a leak on the median strip. You could hear the *whoosh* of beer can flip tops opening, like soft audible fireflies here, there and everywhere in the humid August air.

Squealing sirens and flashing lights of red-and-white EMT vans tried in vain to inch their way through the dust-choked mayhem.

Wunder Mart guards had early-on been tipped off by the state police to clear out every aisle and move the customers outside. They immediately had multiple skirmishes on their hands, notably at the check-out counters. Customers were waiting behind massive cage-carts filled with mounds of two-liter plastic bottles of Mountain Dew and Coke, on sale at two shrink-wrapped-six-packs-for-the-price-of-one, had been advertised all week. The shoppers wouldn't budge. One donnybrook after another broke out.

When the guards finally herded most out into the parking lot, and the customers were told they had to stay put, impromptu tailgate parties erupted. Hibachi grills were fired up. Burgers and dogs were soon sizzling. One family in a brand-new Dodge Ram pickup with Georgia license plates started passing out what they called hillbilly margaritas—cheap tequila with Mountain Dew on the rocks in a Mason jar.

An enterprising, clean-cut young man in a blue blazer—evidently an up-and-coming mid-level manager—rallied the small army of senior-citizen official Wunder Mart greeters and assembled them at all entrances to the parking lot. The smiling greeters continued issuing cheerful welcomes and on-sale coupons to incoming vehicles, whose rude drivers mostly blew past them on the way to what some radio reports were calling a "developing massive police shoot-out. Stayed tuned."

A platoon of video cameras made its way through the boisterous crowd, led by intrepid and recognizable talking-head bronzed anchormen and weather girls in full war paint—from Boston WCVB channel 5, WBZ channel 4, WHDH channel 7, Boston 25; from Providence WPRI channel 12 and WJAR channel 10. All were on the scene. They were catnip to the swarming mob.

"Does anyone know what's going on?" asked a man from Nashua.

"Police won't tell us," replied a woman in a Wunder Mart vest with a name tag reading *I'm Tiffany*!

"Looks like some kind of stand-off situation," declared a man from Brockton.

Hearsay sped through the crowd that there were armed resisters held up somewhere on the sprawling retail playground.

"My sister-in-law works in housewares," a woman from Attleboro said. "She thinks they might have em cornered on the roof."

"My guess it's them ICY-type terrorists," Brockton chimed in.

"Or those MS-13 assholes!" offered a man from Holyoke, almost gleefully.

"I knew it—I just fuckin *knew* it!" said a man from Fitchburg. "Just like Rush warned us."

"Shoot the bastards!" someone yelled from the back of the crowd.

"But how did they *get* here?" a woman from Norwood asked.

"Prob'ly them caravans comin cross the border. You know, the ones we been hearin bout," Holyoke said.

"Wow. All the way from Mexico—how scary is that?" Norwood exclaimed.

"That's what I heard. And worse. They ain't stoppin at nothing," added Brockton.

"What's their plan?" someone cried out.

"Their plan? Their *plan?*" said Holyoke, obviously annoyed at the collective ignorance assembled around him. "Their goddamn plan is to invade us and *take over.*"

"Lock em up!" someone else hollered from the back.

"Whad'ya think they're after?" came another voice.

"Look around—we're talkin the land of plenty with a capital P. They live in absolute shitholes. Don't even use toilet paper. Here they got plastic swimming pools, lawn ornaments, bags of bark, you name it."

"Maybe some a them gangs direct from Iran are sneaking down from Montreal, too," Brockton couldn't resist speculating aloud. "Maybe they're linkin up with the Mescans. Some kinda international conspiracy. Oldest trick in the book. Close in from both sides. Just like a giant boa constrictor."

"Bafor ya know," Holyoke added. "We're all being told no booze on weekends."

"Or worse," said Fitchburg. "No booze at all. They'll have us drinkin goat's milk."

"I'd never thought of that!" a woman from Pawtucket said, eyes wide. "I never did like goats. One nearly bit off my pinky at the Roger Williams Park Zoo when I was five. I mean, I've always thought of them as terrorists."

"Well, we need to *start* thinking," said Holyoke, waving his arms in alarm. "Ya can't trust them Canadians, neither. Talk about sanctuary cities. Don't even use real dollars no more. Somethin called the Loonie. Real joke. Play money if ya ask me. Plus, they answer to the Queen. She calls the shots from the sideline, from one of them big palaces over there."

"You think? My gawd!"

"That's what they say."

Years ago, Holyoke had been stopped at the border in his wife's station wagon. Three or four cases of Budweiser, can-by-can, had been hidden in the door panels and wheel wells. Canadian customs didn't take kindly to his excuse that Moosehead by the bottle was too expensive owing to rampant socialism north of the border.

Overhead the whirring helicopter took another pass. *Tat-tat-tat-tat.*

"Bomb the hell out of em!" someone shouted.

"How many of em are in there, ya think?"

"Oh, could be just a few—or could be a whole terrorist brigade. One of them 'sleeper cells,' I think they call em."

"You think the state cops know what they're up against?"

"We can only hope. We can only hope."

"Your tax dollars at work."

Lieutenant Frank Sullivan and Trooper Julie Egan were part of the law enforcement cluster behind the Wunder Mart. A dozen cop cars and SUVs, more than 20 officers on the ground and one Twin Star helicopter were now preparing to depart the scene.

The suspect had been cuffed and was standing between two troopers next to one of the state SUVs. The man was now wearing orange Crocs, a towel around his waist that came down below his knees, and the blue- mirror sunglasses.

"Tell me again *how* you found out about this?" Sullivan said to Trooper Julie. She studied her senior officer's face and said nothing.

"Was it Cabbie Jack?" Sullivan added.

Egan smiled, removed her own sunglasses, crooked a finger and motioned for Sullivan to lean closer. He did.

"Anonymous phone tip," she whispered. "Told me to go find Aquaman."

40

YOU WILL FIND GOLD

"Trooper Egan," the dispatcher's voice crackled over the patrol car radio. "Return to barracks immediately. The colonel wants to see you."

"Ten-four."

Only days after the fortunately small explosive event, followed by the media and shoppers' circus at the Wunder Mart, a crowd of maybe a couple hundred people filled one parking lot outside the Fox Bowl.

Julie Egan had been driven to the site by Lieutenant Frank Sullivan. As she stepped out of the cruiser, the theme music from *Titanic* blared out of loudspeakers positioned near the main entrance and flagpole.

Jack the Cabbie was seated on a folding chair in the front row, dressed in a white-and-red seersucker suit with matching Panama straw hat and a pencil-thin Boston Blackie false mustache.

The owner of the Pirates was at the podium. Streams of pontificating platitudes poured forth. Several minutes later he finally got to the point, finishing with, "And so, my fellow gridiron aficionados, I have something special for this alert young woman who braved it all to help save Pirates football for the *second* time in half a century.

"Now, madam governor, if you would do the honors. . . ."

The governor of the Commonwealth of Massachusetts stepped up, pulled a spray-painted gold cord and a violet velvet sheet dropped to the stage, revealing a gleaming, full-size golden statue of Biff Bradley.

Arm extended overhead in classic pose, the Adonis of Foxborough frozen forever in pigskin-launch mode. On the base of the custom sculpture was a quote from the philosopher Joseph Campbell: *Where you stumble and fall, there you will find gold.*

Mr. Big said, "Now you'll never be without your very own Biff."

To the crowd's hearty applause, hoots and whistles, Trooper Julie Egan approached the microphone.

She took a long swig from her emergency translucent plastic water bottle filled with vodka, then said, weakly, "I'm speechless."

Off to one side not far from the stage, Mr. Big's driver and bodyguard, both dressed in black and wearing dark aviator sunglasses, leaned against the limo. Mr. Big's septuagenarian personal assistant, Miss Mckenna, was already back in the limo.

Mitch, the limo driver, took a last drag on his Marlboro, flicked the butt and ground it out with his shiny black tasseled loafer.

"Well, the old man finally got rid of that goddamn thing. He sent it to Bradley on his 40th birthday party two years ago. Biffy Boy sent it back. Along with a note that the statue was an *inch too short.*"

41

A SHAUNTAY DAY

Shauntay was reclining for her bi-weekly at Madam Nhu's Tigress Pedicure Palace & Wine Bar, the flagship spa among a series of popular destinations in strip malls throughout the Greater Boston area: Asian Angels in Natick, Smiley Face For You in Milton, Lovely Ladies of the Lily in Waltham, Tiny Touches and Feathery Fantasies in Wellesley, and A Taste of the Rose Petal in Lynn.

She hit redial on her phone for Whitey.

"I appreciate your call," the all-too-familiar recorded voice announced. "I am away for a short spell mentoring underprivileged third-world children. Talk later, merci."

Not 30-minutes later, the fully tricked-out white Range Rover pulled up to Whitey's condo in Quincy. The female driver was out of the car and inside the building's lobby in a few, very quick steps.

"Not here, Miss Shauntay," Eduardo the doorman greeted her. "Mr. LeBlanc, he not here."

My sweet ass he's not here, she thought, eyes and lips narrowing.

Eduardo called upstairs. "Uhm, I think at this time, Mr. LeBlanc he has company."

"I'll bet he does."

Marching briskly across the tiled beige lobby, heels clicking and color-coordinated Hermes 2002 magnolia-pink calfskin bag on her shoulder, Shauntay pushed the up button.

And waited.

When the door opened on the fifth floor, she could smell her! The sickly-sweet trailer trash scent of that Darlene chick Whitey had picked up at the Braintree Mall and swore he would never see again.

"Oh, Antoine," this and "Oh, Antoine," that. Darlene told him whatever he wanted to hear. Shauntay couldn't stand the obsequious little slut.

Using her own key, she let herself in. Subtle noises were coming from the bedroom. She crept around the corner to see the door slightly ajar. The shadow of female figure wearing a football helmet and Whitey's jersey. Darlene was on top and moving up and down rhythmically.

"Oh, Antoine. Oh, oh, oh. . . ."

"Tell me what you want, baby. You know I love to hear it."

"Go deep, Antoine, oh my *god*, go deep."

Reaching into her luxury handbag, then extending her arm, the intruder said aloud, "Have a Shauntay day—you skank!" She spit it out loudly enough so they could both hear her clearly.

Then the lacquered-nail forefinger pulled the silver trigger.

Outside, down on the street a half-a-block away, a purple lowrider van painted with full glitter-gold driver and passenger doors and a custom gold grill sat idling at a stoplight. The van was rocking up and down from side to side, the pavement—the very air—throbbing to the monotonous driving beat of rapper Roy Al Flush:

Hos to the left a me

Hos to da right

Hos be squealin

When yo Big Roy Al

Be lickin hos' toes

Boom, bubba boom, bubba BOOM BOOM BOOM!

A retired Methodist couple from Boothbay Harbor, Maine, both wearing sensible shoes and traveling in a sensible Buick sedan with a steamed lobster on the license plate stenciled Vacationland slowly pulled up behind the vibrating purple van.

The Buick stopped and the quiet couple was facing the back door of the van, which sported a colorful sticker of the Puerto Rican flag and read *51st STATE!*

Below the flag was a taped-on spray-painted piece of cardboard:

DOLL, U GOT

BRASIL BUTT LIFT??????

I'M IN!!!!!!!!

TEXT ANGEL NOW

The traffic light turned green, the van moved forward when Angel, the 21-year-old at the wheel, gunned it. He accelerated, steering with his knees, both hands free, thumb and fingers dancing over his phone screen.

In a perfectly choreographed 30 seconds, just when Shauntay was squeezing the trigger on her 9mm Luger, the whole room exploded.

BOOOOOM!

A searing white fireball blew out the window. Blue and white smoke and pieces of mattress rained down five stories. Fragments of football trophies hit the sidewalk like metallic confetti. A flaming souvenir Pirates throw pillow followed.

Turns out the Fox Bowl wasn't the only place set up to blow.

Angel's 19-year-old cousin, Juan, in the passenger seat, took another hit of his joint just as a Realistic Sexy Female Mannequin from LA ("Fast Shipping in the USA!" "Human

Customer Support!" "7-Day Moneyback Return!") plummeted down and hit the van's off-road grill guard.

Hit it hard. *So hard* and with such ferocity, that the four-pound two-ounce Riddell Revolution Speed authentic NFL football helmet, Tru-Curve aggressive shell constructed of polycarbonate material, with polyvinyl-coated steel facemask, four-point chin strap, and full interior snap-out padding, bounced skyward—torso wearing only the jersey; shapely legs naked.

But neither Angel nor his cousin knew the body they had just hit was polyurethane and foam rubber.

"H-o-l-y f-u-c-k-i-n SHIT!" Juan yelled, wide-eyed.

"Mother of Jesus," said Angel, hitting the brakes momentarily and glancing in his rearview mirror.

"What we tell the cops?" Juan cried.

"I don't know, broki, but I ain't waitin' aroun' find out," Angel said, adrenaline pumping and his heart beating like it was coming through his throat. He slammed his foot on the gas pedal. The purple van fishtailed, tires squealing as it disappeared into traffic.

A split-second after the inflatable dummy had flown over the roof of the van, it rocketed past the driver's side of the sensible Buick sedan, oil changed punctually every 3,000 miles back to home in Maine at the Good N You Fuel & Service.

"You see that, Arvin?" the woman passenger said.

"Aye-yah, Martha, suppose I did. Couldn't help noticin."

The Buick moved forward, slowly. Perhaps a full five-seconds went by when the woman added; "Arvin, do you think we should stop and go back? You know, see if anything's the matt-ah?"

"Wouldn't worry none, Martha. Young-stahs just havin sum fun, likely. Must be sum kinda football good luck for the big team down he-ah," he said. "They shore do spend time dressin up for them Pirates. And must drop some real money, too. Aye-yah."

More silence. Arvin watched the traffic in both directions.

"See em on the TV. Colored wigs and all. Pirate tattoos. Six-foot swords. Must dip themselves in a hot-tub of paint the day a'fore each game. Twenty degrees out. Snowin," he said, shaking his head.

"And to see the girls dressed that way, too," Martha nodded with an audible sigh.

"Ya know, Chester down't the pancake house won a pair of playoff tickets at that Fox Bowl place a few years back, I think from the Brunswick Rotary Club," Arvin said. "Bought a raffle ticket. Treated him and Mabel to a big weekend. Put them up in one of them $99-a-night motels with the free breakfast."

"Turns out the tickets were worth $595 apiece. Chester, he looked it up. Couldn't hardly believe it. Right above the 50-yard line. Guess they didn't see much. Shame. Drove all that way. Seats were right behind this fella who kept jumpin up and down, howlin and yellin, to beat the band. Aye-yah," Arvin said, pausing to remember exactly how he heard the story.

"Great big guy. Naked from the waist up. Had one of those miniature horses in the seat next to him. Dyed tail and mane—matchin. Horse was wearing an eye patch and three-corner hat."

"My land!" Martha gasped.

Seconds passed before he spoke again.

"Martha," he said.

"Yes, Arvin?"

"Let's thank the good Lord our Red Sox ain't come to that."

42

ABSOLUTE MAGIC

"We are now at cruising altitude," the reassuring voice said over the cabin speakers. "I'm captain Sonny Hawkins and pleased to be your pilot today. Beside me is co-pilot-in-training B. T. "Butch" Bagley. We call him "the Bag Handler"—just in case, you know, this sleek beauty decides to take us on a surprise tour over the pyramids and Butch has to take over. *Which*, by the way, you'll be pleased to know that we *could* reach without refueling. Midnight camel ride, anyone? Hey-hey-hey. . . ."

"Roger that!" Butch said.

The captain then told his three passengers that this new G500 features state of the art Pratt & Whitney engines with a range of 5,200 nautical miles at Mach 0.85.

"We expect to be touching down in Bermuda in about two hours. While you fine folks are enjoying the warm ocean breeze, the sand and the beautiful bougainvillea, Butch will be at St. David's Island practicing his takeoffs and landings. Gotta stay sharp."

"Roger that!"

"Meantime, sit back, allow our attentive crew to serve you a delicious beverage while you enjoy 100 percent clean, fresh air replenished every two minutes. Another happy reason to never fly commercial again."

Gabriella Sophia Bonita tapped her phone and dialed the beach house. A maid picked up. "Anita—is my Biff there?"

The young woman's voice on the other end said, "No, missy, Mister Bradley, he in iz *Zuuum*ba class."

"Never should have introduced him to Beto," she mused with a smirk, referring to the Columbian-born dancer and choreographer Alberto Pérez, now the toast of the idle wives of Miami Beach.

Gabriella put down her copy of *Vanity Fair*, unbuckled her seat belt, rose from the hand-stitched humanely harvested gazelle leather seat ("The G500 helps passengers achieve true cabin bliss through attention to detail and personal styling!") and slid aft in her bare feet over the cashmere carpeting.

"Whitey," the former Miss Universe said. "We should talk."

"Suppose so," said Antoine LeBlanc, Jr., rising half way out of his own seat in the rear of the cabin.

"Brandi," said LeBlanc, "would you please excuse us?" It was the Dunkin drive-thru chick! Still frosty blonde with purple and pink stripes. And tats. Tit tats.

"Of course, baby," touching Whitey's shaved head, adjusting her ear buds and discreetly disappearing into the cockpit.

Gabriella took Brandi's seat. "Look," she said, "I know this didn't work out."

"Say *that* again!" Whitey exclaimed with a sigh. "A real cluster-fuck."

"Nobody got hurt," Gabriella said.

"There's that," he said. "But you're out a million bucks."

She shrugged and waved her long, slender fingers: *"Lo que fácil viene, fácil se va."*

"It's a million fuckin bucks!" he repeated, still not quite believing it, letting it sink in. "And for what?"

"Whitey, dear, I used to make that in two weeks."

"Shit," he said, emotionally deflated.

"It's not the money. The *real* issue here is how we get Biff off the field—for good," she said. "You were his favorite receiver. He'll listen to you."

"He ain't goin until he is forced to."

"That's what worries me. There are limits to the magic of avocado face cream. I don't want to see him carried off the field on a stretcher."

"Yeah. Happens too often. Gettin worse."

"It's a miracle he's lasted this long."

"He's got his pride."

"What we've got to do is figure out a way to allow him to exit with a big bang," she said, pausing momentarily with a wince at the irony. "You know—big show."

"What if he calls his shot?" Whitey asked, perking up. "Like the Babe."

"Who's that?"

"Babe Ruth. Most famous baseball player who ever lived. Practically invented it. 'The national pastime,' they used to call it. Until Joe Namath slipped into pantyhose on game day and stole America's sports-crazy heart. Ain't never been the same. . . ."

Whitey told Gabriella that it had to be orchestrated at home, at the Bowl, place filled with 60,000 screaming fans; first game of the season, first quarter. Build this whole thing up to a crescendo: Biff Go Deep, Biff Go Deep, *Biff Go Deep!*

"Maybe the whole social media deal," he said. "A website. Billboards. Talk-show call-ins. T-shirts. Full-size cardboard cutouts. One a them crowdsourcing things." *Hmmm. Now there's a way to hide some serious incoming bucks. Obfuscate the donor trail.*

The end result, Whitey explained, would be to whip hundreds of thousands—shit, why not *millions?*—of Biff fanatics into a collective frenzy over something that they imagined would be big, but without quite knowing what's coming. But they'll convince themselves that it's something truly spectacular.

"It has to be a crazy ass long throw—50, 60 yards out, right into the end zone and a pair of supine waiting arms. Just reaches up and snags the ball, maybe with one hand. The defending receivers take just a couple steps off their pace. Make it look legit."

A flight attendant appeared: "Something to drink?"

"Bourbon rocks—Rebel Yell, if ya got it," Whitey said.

"Moroccan mint green tea, small batch, free-trade, double organic," Gabriella said, eyeing the cardboard box of Dunkin Munchkin hole treats Brandi had brought along.

"The announcers will never buy it," she said, skeptically. "I've watched enough games."

"And I've *been in* enough games. Listen, those jargon-spouting ex-jocks will instantly know a spectacular play when they see it."

Whitey pulled out a pad and pen and started scribbling:

I SENSE SOMETHING BIG'S COMING

BRADLEY AT MID-FIELD

YOU'RE RIGHT—ANYTHING CAN HAPPEN

AND USUALLY DOES
THERE'S THE SNAP
RECEIVERS ARE ROLLING RIGHT
THEY'RE GOING DEEP
THE CROWD IS GOING WILD
BRADLEY IS POINTING
HE'S CALLING HIS SHOT!
DO YOU BELIEVE IT?
THERE IT GOES
HAVE YOU EVER SEEN SUCH A MISSLE?
IT'S AN ABSOLUTE BOMB
THE RECEIVER LIES DOWN, REACHES UP AND
SNARES IT!
INCREDIBLE!!!!!
UNBELEIVABLE!!!!!
THIS PLACE IS EXPLODING
IT'S A PLAY FOR THE AGES
I WOULD'T TRADE PLACES WITH ANYONE,
ANYWHERE
WE'RE WATCHING HISTORY, PARTNER
I JUST THANK THE GOOD LORD THAT HE
PUT ME HERE
YOU AND ME BOTH, BUDDY
IT'S BREATHTAKING
WHAT WILL WE TELL THE GRANDKIDS?

IT'S OVERWHELMING
I'M SPEECHLESS
ABSOLUTE MAGIC
I WAS THERE—SAYS IT ALL
WE WERE THERE WHEN BIFF BRADLEY CALLED HIS SHOT
WHAT COULD EVER TOP THIS?
A MIRACLE?
IT WOULD HAVE TO BE A PRETTY BIG ONE

The former Miss Universe read down the list. First a smile, then her eyes twinkled.

Whitey: "We have this typed up in large letters and printed out on fancy Pirates stationery. Get every announcer in the place boozed-up an hour before kickoff and then have some Pirates cheerleaders run around to all the broadcast booths and hand each of these slick boys an embossed envelope. Make it look like it came directly from Mr. Big. But don't hand it to them until opening kickoff."

Gabriella: "Any note or instructions?"

"No."

"How are they going to know what it means?"

Whitey: "They're not. But the instant the whole stunt starts ta unfold before their eyes, and they look down at all these clichés, there ain't no way these stupid motherfuckers gonna be able to resist shouting all this shit into the mic. They'll run right down the list. Swept up in the moment. *Yee-hah!*"

"So, they sell the whole thing to 60,000 people?"

"Sixty thousand? Hah! And millions on live TV—not to mention the endless YouTube replays." Whitey got more animated.

Tipping back another mouthful of golden-brown elixir, he went on. "Can't leave nothin to chance. The refs suspend the game. Biff strolls off the field in that lanky gait and disappears down the runway. The crowd starts chanting: Biff Go Deep! *Biff Go Deep!*

"Okay, game resumes. The panicked announcers are hurling wild speculation: 'Is this the end? Is he hurt? What's your take? Courtney, any report from the locker room?'

"Halftime whistle blows," Whitey acted out, arms up indicating stop the clock. "The grounds crew gates open and out comes Biff Bradley riding a golden Roman chariot pulled by eight white horses!"

The decibels, Whitey assured her, "will be deafening."

"Oh, my God," Gabriella said, brown eyes widening. "The Roman Colosseum?

"Damn straight—Charlton Heston and Kirk Douglas, baby! Jes pitcher your conquering hero circling the Fox Bowl and waving to the crazed crowd. I mean, beats hell out of the goofy duck boat parade."

"I suppose you could be bringing up the rear in your cute yellow convertible," she offered."

Whitey paused. He hadn't thought of that. "Hey, why not?" he said, in a flash imagining himself back in the spotlight again. And not thinking that the Mass. State Police had more than likely already impounded the lone vehicle owned by Bayou Business Enterprises, LLC.

"I certainly got the right plates!" *The ultimate finger to the Pirates. Right in the belly of the beast. Oh, too perfect, too perfect. . . .*

"Then, the moment of truth," Whitey continued. The Fox Bowl explodes in fireworks and Mr. Big emerges Mick Jagger-style from a cloud of blue smoke and gold glitter, Biff by his side, superlatives shamelessly echoing over acres of hushed humanity, announcing the legendary quarterback's eternal retirement. Pirates cheerleaders come rolling out with a humungous rhinestone "Key to the Fox Bowl."

"Let me guess. Tears are flowing and Biff says he's the luckiest man alive. . . ."

"No, no, no. Not that Lou Gehrig thing. Can't do that. Would be good, though."

"Who's Lou?"

"Another dead Yankee. Biff deserves something original."

"Then we'd have to get a real speechwriter. Fly him in from Hollywood. Not a problem. I know half a dozen who would do it for free—for the honor."

She picked up her phone and called her personal secretary back in New York: "Trevor, darling, would you see if Biff Go Deep dot com is available—you know, the internet domain?

"What if it's taken?" said the perfectly enunciated, clipped British voice on the other end.

"Then call Cupertino and steal it. I won't take no for an answer. And Trevor. . . ."

"Yes, ma'am?"

"Keep your mouth shut."

"You have my ultimate discretion, as always. And, ma'am, do you want dot net, too?"

The trim, vivacious Colombian with the light-olive skin placed the phone in her lap. She looked out the Gulfstream's light-flooded panoramic window to the blue Atlantic below.

"I must say, Whitey, I can see it," she said. "But one problem, bright guy. How on earth do you *guarantee* that sensational touchdown?"

"Biff's still got the arm. Don't believe any of that bullshit that he's lost it."

"No, not *Biff*—the coaches, the refs, the opposing team?"

Whitey looked at her with vacant eyes, as if to say: *Really? You're kidding, right?*

Whitey held up his thumb and first two fingers and rubbed them together in a miniature massage of make-believe dollars. He lifted his glass and crunched the last of the melted ice in his teeth.

"Money?" she said. "Is that all it would take to make this wild spectacle possible? You're telling me the *whole League* can be bought?"

"Gabby," Whitey said slowly, smirk turning to gleaming smile. "Does Coach Willy wear a hoodie?"

MEET THE AUTHORS

Terry Boone is a native of West Virginia. At the age of nine, listening to basketball and baseball broadcasts, he knew that he wanted to work in radio. Family lore quotes his paternal grandfather: "Kid doesn't need training. Let's just put a knob on him so we can turn him off once in a while."

News reporting, DJ, advertising, management and all the things that small-market broadcasters do, led to station ownership and the launch of one of Northern New England's first "eclectic-alternative" music stations, WKXE in White River Junction, Vermont.

Recipient of numerous reporting, editorial, programming and management awards (West Virginia, Massachusetts, New Hampshire and Vermont), Boone has generally tried to stay out of the way of more talented broadcast associates, while attempting to provide the support and resources required to satisfy a loyal audience.

In 2014, with the publication of *A Cold Morning in Maine*, the New England Mysteries series was introduced. Hence, a pretty good storyteller aspiring to become a better writer. Six books along and here we are, having a beer and clams at the Red Wing Diner.

Thomas R. Pero was born in Fall River, Massachusetts and raised in Taunton. He was just 18 when he started the Southeastern Massachusetts Chapter of Trout Unlimited, the youngest chapter president ever. At age 23, he was named editor of *Trout* magazine, which twice during his 16-year tenure was named Conservation Magazine of the Year by the Natural Resources Council of America.

In 2010 Pero was awarded the Starker Leopold Wild Trout Metal at the Wild Trout Symposium in Yellowstone for a lifetime of influential writing about coldwater fisheries conservation.

His 2016 book, *Gettysburg 1863—Seething Hell*, received the prestigious Benjamin Franklin Award from the world's largest association of independent publishers for the best book about American history published that year.

Today, Pero writes the Outdoor Adventures column for *Business Jet Traveler* magazine. Years ago, when trying to track down an elusive Ted Williams for an interview while salmon fishing on the Miramichi River in Canada, Williams growled, "You've probably heard I don't like writers."

"I know," replied Pero, "but I fish." He got the interview.

SIGNED COPIES

For copies of *Go Deep* signed by the authors,
go to the book's website: www.biffgodeep.com

Three Rivers Group, Post Office Box 885, Norwich,
Vermont 05055 USA—telephone 802-238-9393

Wild River Press, Post Office Box 13360, Mill Creek,
Washington 98082 USA—telephone 425-486-3638

Distributed to the book trade by
Independent Publishers Group, Chicago

Acknowledgments

Sympathy for the Devil The Rolling Stones (12/68—Decca)
Buckle Down, Winsocki Tommy Dix/Chorus (11/43—MGM)
Theme for Jaws John Williams (6/75—MCA)
The Tide is High Blondie (10/80—Chrysalis)
Every Breath You Take The Police (5/83—A & M)
Material Girl Madonna (1/85—Sire-Warner Bros)
Theme from A Summer Place Percy Faith (9/59—Columbia)
Chariots of Fire Vangelis (5/81—Polydor)
Looney Tunes Theme (11/47—Warner Bros)
Bonanza David Rose Orchestra (10/59—MGM)
Dragnet Ray Anthony (10/53—Capitol)
The River Kwai March and Col. Bogey Mitch Miller (1/58—Columbia)
Gonna Fly Now Bill Conti (4/77—United Artists)
Brother Love's Travelling Salvation Show Neil Diamond (2/69—Uni)
Eastern War Dance Narragansett Indian Tribe Pow Wow
Wooly Bully Sam The Sham and The Pharaohs (4/65—MGM)
The Next Episode Dr. Dre & Snoop Dogg (4/00—Aftermath)
My Heart Will Go On Celine Dion (12/97—Columbia/Epic)

The Thomas Crown Affair (6/68—United Artists)
Patton (2/70—20th Century Fox)
Aquaman (11/18—Warner Bros)

Thank you for the music *and* the movies!

◊ ◊ ◊

Red Wing Diner—www.redwingdiner.com
Dunkin Donuts—www.dunkinathome.com
Old Canteen—www.theoldcanteen.com
Narragansett Indian Tribe of Rhode Island—
www.narragansettindiannation.org